D0387325

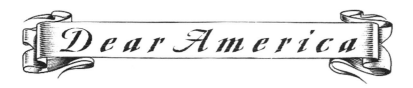

Mirror, Mirror on the Wall

The Diary of Bess Brennan

BY BARRY DENENBERG

Scholastic Inc.   New York

Boston, Massachusetts

1932

Sunday, December 27, 1931

I don't know what I would do without Elin, my twin sister.

Writing my diary for me is her idea. She knows how faithful I've been. I haven't missed one single, solitary day since I was seven, which is almost five years ago.

I can remember the last entry I wrote:

The snow continued to fall throughout the night. It appears as if the whole earth is carpeted in white — a truly glorious sight. Elin and I are going sledding before anyone else ruins the pristine snowfall.

Elin insists we can do it together. We do everything else together, she says, so why not this?

We're in my room now and Elin is writing all this down.

Elin and I are mirror twins: I'm left-handed and

Elin is right-handed so when we face each other and move, it's like seeing yourself in a mirror.

Elin thinks I ought to talk about the accident first, so I shall.

It was early on the morning of December fifth and we were sledding down the big hill behind the boarded-up Baldwin house. It was a perfect day for sledding: sunny, not too cold. The freshly fallen, untouched snow blanketed the entire hill.

Unfortunately, just after we arrived, Brian McManus and some of his friends came and started sledding right next to us, which was most annoying because there was ample room for them elsewhere on the hill. Of course this came as no surprise because if there's one word that describes Brian McManus it's annoying. He's in our class even though he's older. In the entire history of Arlington Junior High, he's the only one who's been left back twice.

Every time we went down the hill one of them would follow in our wake, yelling like a hyena and purposely coming closer each time, just to scare us.

On my third run Brian came right at me, grinning that foolish grin he always wears. I veered sharply to the right to avoid the inevitable collision and I didn't see the tree until it was too late. I don't even remember hitting the tree, just seeing it rushing toward me like it was moving and not me.

The next thing I remember was waking up in a strange bed and wondering why my eyes were all bandaged.

After that, nothing was ever the same.

I spent countless hours in the crowded waiting room at the Mass. General Eye Clinic wondering if they were ever going to call my name and if they made the seats that hard on purpose.

I endured tedious examinations by doctors in starched coats that crinkled when they moved and who came so close to my face that I could smell their medicine smell.

They dripped drops in my eyes that they said dilated my pupils but only burned. They flashed lights in my eyes. I could see only a milky white cloud — the snow, I thought.

They scratched notes on pads and had low-voiced conversations with Mama and Uncle Ted: "very serious condition," "detached retinas," "experimental but urgent operations," "odds are against us," "nothing we can do."

I had two operations in two weeks.

When the bandages were removed after the first operation I could see enough to know if someone was there. Sparks of light appeared when I closed my eyes.

The worst part was having to lie completely still: They had something on either side of my head to keep me from moving. I had to lie that way for days.

I remember waking up not knowing what time it was or even what day, and realizing Elin had fallen asleep in the chair but was still holding my hand. Or hearing the sound of Mama furiously knitting away as she kept her night vigil by my side.

After each operation, my sight worsened. In the beginning, I was able to tell when it was day and when it was night. But after the second operation, I couldn't even do that.

What little vision I had right after the accident was slowly evaporating until a dark curtain descended, letting in the barest amount of light.

I needed a miracle, not an operation. The operations failed and the miracle never came.

Elin claims she isn't tired but I am, so I will continue tomorrow.

It's me, Elin. Bess is sound asleep. I'm so happy she's letting me do this for her. She has always been so good about her diary. No matter how late it was, or how early we had to get up in the morning, she wouldn't go to sleep until she finished that day's entry.

That's how I got the idea.

The night Bess came home after her last operation, I noticed that there was no light coming from under her door. I had gotten so used to seeing her light while she scribbled away in her diary that I was startled by its absence. Ever since the accident, I had been trying to think of anything I could do to make her feel better. Surely, I thought, there must be something. But no matter how hard I concentrated I couldn't think of anything.

Walking down the hall that night I realized there was something. I could help her keep her diary. I could write it down for her. I wasn't sure if Bess would like my idea. Maybe she would think that a diary wasn't truly a diary if someone else was hearing everything you said. If you can't be totally honest, is it a real diary?

But when I suggested it, Bess brightened up for the first time since the accident. She wanted to try. She said if there was anyone in the world she didn't mind knowing her innermost thoughts, it was me.

It was her idea that I write in it, also. Frankly I'd rather not. For one thing, I'm not a very good writer — certainly not as good as my sister. And it just doesn't seem right — but Bess insists, so here I am.

Hearing Bess talk about that awful morning was the first time I truly understood what happened. It was all so quick. One moment I was watching her sledding down the hill and the next moment everything was a blur: the terrifying ride in the back of the ambulance while it screamed through the traffic; the frustrating confusion in the emergency room; explaining everything to Mama and Uncle Ted when they, at last, arrived; seeing the stricken look in Mama's eyes; trying to understand what the doctors were saying and not believing what I was hearing.

And then, later, sitting there with Bess. She was so patient — I don't know how she did it. If it had been me, I would have jumped out of my skin. Hour after hour in brightly lit, overheated waiting rooms filled with people, and wondering what their troubles were. And worse, hour after hour in those dreadful hospital rooms.

Bess wanted me to be with her so I came every time. Both times she had to go into the hospital for those operations we all put our faith in, despite the doctors' measured words of caution. And every time she went to see them about her progress afterwards.

God, how she hated those doctors. She said she could accept their uncertainty but not their unwillingness to admit it. She said nothing when they asked her if she had any questions because she knew they just wanted to move on to the next patient.

At least I could be there and listen to her. I'm a very good listener, like Mama.

Monday, December 28, 1931

I am relieved to be home but my sorrow is unfathomable.

There is so much that I will never see again, so much I have taken for granted: Mama's garden; the smoke from Uncle Ted's pipe; the late afternoon sun casting its purple-orange glow on the front porch swing; my dear sister's face.

There will be no more "Mirror, mirror on the wall."

Ever since we were little, Elin and I would stand in front of the hall mirror and say: "Mirror, mirror on the wall, who in the realm is the fairest of all?" And then I would say, "You are," and Elin would say, "I am," and we would laugh and laugh and laugh.

Mama is quite beside herself. She's continually baking. Every day there's a different pie on the kitchen table.

Elin says that's what she did when Daddy passed on, although I don't know how she can possibly remember because we were only four years old.

I asked Mama if I could help her bake, like I always do, but she said she was all finished.

Mama was never much of a talker, but now she's as quiet as a mouse.

I asked Bess if she wanted me to read my entries to her, so that it would be fair. After all, I get to hear everything that she's saying. But Bess thought it would be better if I kept mine private because she's used to keeping a diary and telling the truth, but I might not write down the real truth if I knew anyone was going to read it.

She's probably right.

She's certainly right about Mama's baking. If it doesn't stop soon, or at least slow down, we're going to have to hang up a sign and get a cash register. That's what Uncle Ted said, but not in front of Mama or Bess, just me.

Bess doesn't believe that I really, really remember Mama baking when Daddy passed on, but I do. I remember all of it: waking up in the

morning and finding Uncle Ted in the kitchen; listening to him explaining that Mama and Daddy had to run an errand and knowing
that it wasn't the truth and that something bad was going to happen.

That's what makes Bess and I so different. Bess never remem-
bers anything bad and I never forget.

Tuesday, December 29, 1931

Uncle Ted told me I won't be able to go back to
Arlington School.

I know I shouldn't have been surprised by this but
I was.

He said there is a school nearby that teaches only
blind children. I told him I don't want to go to school
with blind children. I want to go to school with
Elin. I have always gone to school with Elin. I told
him I didn't want to talk about it anymore.

Wednesday, December 30, 1931

Bess didn't want to write anything today. She's too upset about
school. She didn't get out of bed and she didn't eat anything the
whole day.

I haven't been to school since the accident. I haven't even thought about it.

Thursday, December 31, 1931

Uncle Ted came to tell me a joke so I knew he wanted to discuss the blind school again.

He visited there yesterday. He said it is bigger than Arlington School and overlooks the Charles River. There are all these redbrick buildings that are covered with ivy, acres and acres of grass, and lots of old oaks, stately maples, and tall pine trees. The cottages where the students live are connected by covered walkways and there's a playground and a pond where kids were ice-skating.

He said they can teach me to read with my fingers, which sounds like quite a trick. I nearly laughed, but Uncle Ted sounded so sad I didn't want to hurt his feelings.

He said the best thing is that it is so close that I can come home every weekend.

Uncle Ted is just like Daddy. He thinks there's a silver lining to every cloud.

Friday, January 1, 1932

I had an awful dream last night.

I dreamt I was standing on a rocky shore looking out over a storm-tossed sea. The ferocious waves were crashing all around me in ever-increasing fury.

I was terrified that soon one of the enormous waves would rise up over my head, engulf me, and drag me out to the vast, angry ocean, forever.

Saturday, January 2, 1932

Elin heard Mama and Uncle Ted talking about me in the kitchen last night and woke me up so I could listen as well.

Mama doesn't want me going to the blind school. She said she would be my eyes, and she would take care of me.

Uncle Ted, patient as always, let Mama speak her mind. But when she was done, he proceeded to tell her all the things about the school he had told me, including reading with your fingers. But then he told her something he hadn't told me. He said the school would teach me to be independent, too, and to be able to take care of myself.

I could tell Mama was crying. She must have been very upset because she said something that I know she didn't mean. She said it was easy for Uncle Ted to send me away because I'm not his daughter.

Uncle Ted isn't easily angered. He said that keeping me home so they could watch me around the clock, do everything for me, and protect me from all harm isn't what is best for me.

"Someday, my dear sister-in-law," he said, "neither of us will be around to hold Bess's hand. What will happen to her then?"

No one spoke for the longest time. It was so quiet we could hear Grandma's clock ticking in the living room.

For the first time since the accident I began to cry.

I don't like to cry. Daddy disapproved of crying. But I couldn't hold it in any longer.

I was crying because of all that has happened to me, but even more because I knew right then that Uncle Ted was right. I always liked doing things for myself and now there is nothing I can do on my own.

I have to go to the blind school. I have to find a way to live my life.

I hope I did the right thing: waking Bess up so she could hear what Mama and Uncle Ted were saying. I didn't tell her about the first part of the conversation. About Uncle Ted going to see Mr. McManus.

Uncle Ted is a blessing. I don't know what we would have done if he hadn't stayed on after Daddy's funeral.

I wish Bess hadn't started crying, and I wish she wasn't going to that blind school.

Friday, January 15, 1932

Elin says I'd better start talking because we have my entire first week at the Perkins School for the Blind to go over and it's already 10:00.

So . . .

Mama said she wanted me to look pretty and feel pretty for my first day at my new school, so she bought me a new dress. "First impressions are lasting impressions," she said.

I think she felt badly that she wasn't going with us, but she needn't.

She was trembling as she hugged me. "Just remember, Bess," she said, "if you don't like it there you don't have to stay. This is your home and nothing on God's green earth will ever change that."

At Perkins, I met Mrs. Burton, my new housemother, and Amanda Bright and Eva Anderson, my new roommates.

Amanda has a deep, throaty voice and is by far the more talkative of the two. She explained that she is a "semi," which means she can see a little. Eva rarely speaks and when she does it's as if each word had a painful price attached to it. She is quite shy, although not unfriendly.

On the way to our room, I stumbled going up the spiral staircase. If it hadn't been for Amanda's steadying hand I might have fallen. She says everyone does that in the beginning. I have never been on a spiral staircase before and being unable to see didn't help matters.

Amanda said we could unpack and put away my clothes later. She wanted to show me how to organize everything so I would know where to find it when I got dressed in the morning. "You know," she said, "so you don't go out looking like a fool."

I hadn't thought about that because Elin and Mama have been laying out my clothes every morning.

Amanda said everyone is back from their Christmas vacations. She just returned from Nantucket where she lives. Nantucket, Amanda explained proudly, is a teeny, tiny island off the coast of Massachusetts. Her father is a fisherman and her grandfather used to hunt for whales.

She pulled me close and whispered not to say anything to Eva about vacations because Eva didn't go anywhere. She has no family and never gets any letters or telephone calls. Amanda said Eva is an orphan.

"Most of the time, new students start in September," Amanda went on, changing subjects when Eva came back from the bathroom. She said the Perkins School made an exception in my case because I live close enough to go home on weekends and could adjust better to the situation.

Amanda seems to know everything there is to know and doesn't mind letting you know she knows.

After a while we had to go downstairs because the supper bell rang. Mrs. Burton wanted to introduce me to the rest of the "blinks." By "blinks," I think Amanda means the other blind girls who live in Bradlee Cottage.

Downstairs, the room was filled with chattering girls. When we entered, Mrs. Burton asked each girl to introduce herself, stating her name, hometown, grade, and best and worst quality.

Mrs. Burton explained that this was a tradition when a new student came to Bradlee Cottage. "So we can all get to know one another truly and better," she said, but sounded like she didn't mean it.

They all claimed such sterling qualities; even their bad ones sounded good. Amanda said her best quality is her sparkling personality and her worst, which took her longer than anyone else to come up with, is biting her nails. Eva said her best quality is her voice, which is true. When she does speak, it's like hearing the ringing of a bell.

I wanted so much to pick something virtuous. Something that would make everyone want to be my friend. However, I didn't want to sound like I was bragging, so I just told the truth.

I told them my best quality is loyalty and my worst, stubbornness.

Then it was time for dinner.

Mrs. Burton explained that, although I would not be required to do anything my first week, "No one is waited on at Perkins, Tess."

I don't know where she got the idea that I expect to be waited on, and I considered telling her my name isn't Tess. But there was so much going on that I didn't have time, nor the presence of mind.

Amanda led me to my place next to her and we stood behind our chairs until Mrs. Burton rang the bell, signaling that we should be seated. When she rang the bell again, everyone said grace, and dinner was served.

I hadn't eaten with anyone besides my family since the accident.

Everyone was passing food back and forth and talking a mile a minute. Amanda had warned me that she had to get up and help with the serving because she was a "semi" ("In the land of the blind, the one-eyed man is king," she whispered) and I should just sit and wait till she returned. Fortunately she was only gone a couple of minutes and just as I was about to panic, she reappeared beside me and put some food on my plate and told me to imagine that my plate was like the face of a clock. She said my pork chops were at six, my potatoes at nine, peas at three, and apple-sauce at one.

I asked her if that was a.m. or p.m.

"Well," Amanda said, betraying a note of genuine surprise, "I guess you'll do fine."

It was good that Mama didn't go with us. She would have been too upset, which would have made it even more difficult. I think Bess wanted us to just drop her off and leave and so we did. When we were driving home, Uncle Ted said he thought so, too.

Bess's roommates sound very nice, which is a big relief because Mrs. Burton wasn't at all friendly and I hated leaving my sister with her.

Bess wanted to know what Mrs. Burton looks like. I'm not very good at describing people and there isn't very much to describe about

Mrs. Burton. Mostly she's plain and black and white. It's like she isn't in color like the rest of us. She has black hair and was wearing a black dress. Her skin is white — not pink or flesh-colored like other people's.

Bess can't wait till I meet Amanda and Eva and can tell her what they look like.

Bess confessed that it was terrifying having to go down to the dining room and meet all those girls without being able to see any of them.

Sunday, January 17, 1932

I know Mama was upset that I didn't go to church with everyone, even though she didn't say anything. I don't want them to look at me, which is precisely what will happen and I won't even know it.

I had trouble sleeping the first night at Perkins. It seemed so dark, although I knew it wasn't any darker than it is at home. When I was little, I made Daddy check the room to make sure no one was hiding anywhere. I wish he could do that for me now.

The room was unbearably hot and stuffy and the

only window had to be kept closed. Amanda said that Eva was scared of getting a sore throat because of her singing.

The harder I tried to go to sleep, the more awake I became. I felt so out of place: in a strange room with two girls I barely knew.

Apparently Amanda was having trouble sleeping, also. She wanted to know if anyone, which I imagine meant Eva or me, knew why Mrs. Burton didn't have a little finger on her right hand.

Undeterred by the lack of response, Amanda said she would tell us but we had to swear not to "spill the beans" to anyone.

"Years ago," she said, "people were afraid of being buried alive so they requested their little finger be cut off to make sure they were indeed dead. That way they would cry out, alerting their loved ones that they were still among the living."

This, according to Amanda, is precisely what happened to Mrs. Burton. She had a seizure of some sort and showed no signs of life. When her family proceeded with the amputation to confirm her death, Mrs. Burton awoke from her stupor with a start, and screamed out in pain, thus narrowly escaping the un-speakable fate of being buried alive.

But not, Amanda added gleefully, in time to save her now-severed finger.

Inexplicably, Amanda's gruesome story made me forget my concerns and I finally fell asleep.

Tuesday night, we organized my clothes. I share the big closet with Eva, while Amanda has the small one all to herself. We each have our own drawers.

All my sweaters and blouses are in one drawer with the darker colors on the bottom and the lighter ones on the top. We hung my clothes dark to light, left to right. "It rhymes," Amanda said, "so you'll never forget." Amanda also showed me how to feel for the buttons to make sure my skirts aren't on backwards and how to tell which shoe goes on which foot.

She has an endless list of suggestions. She calls them "Amanda's Helpful Hints for the Sightless and Semi-sightless." If I ever drop something she said to be quiet and still so I can hear where it falls. And don't ever, ever bend forward to pick anything up —

it's a good way to hit your head. "Squat, don't bend." — Amanda's Survival Rule number 12.

Each day after class, Amanda showed me how to get around by myself. "Learn to love counting steps," she said. "Counting steps is the difference between slavery and freedom." Amanda is quite melodramatic at times.

I have to remember how many steps it is from the cottage to the Howe building and where to go once I'm inside.

She showed me the main hall where there are rows and rows of glass cases filled with dead, stuffed animals: squirrels, monkeys, birds, foxes, and even a cow.

"At Perkins," Amanda said, "they know you can't see the world but they want you to feel the world."

Then we walked down the halls to the library, and the chapel. She showed me how to use my hands to feel along the wall and the banister. She warned me not to get upset when I unexpectedly bang into something. "It's a blessing in disguise," she said. "It's the only way you'll know something's there."

Amanda said after a while, when I become a little

more comfortable, I should try snapping my fingers as I walk down the halls of the Howe building. I should see if I can tell the difference in the sounds as I go. She told me not to give up if nothing happens for a long time. My hearing will get better each day and then, one day, I'll just hear and that will be the beginning.

Back outside, she said I should pay attention to the ground beneath my feet at all times. Was I on the brick walkway or had I wandered off onto the grass? Where was the edge of the lawn? The edge of a curb? Was there a tree root rising up through the cobblestones that could serve as a landmark?

I don't think I will ever learn to walk around Perkins on my own. It's simply too big and too confusing.

I was all right for the first couple of days, but Thursday afternoon Amanda said she would follow behind me to see how I would do on my own.

After a while, I was sure I had gone the wrong way. I became nervous, stricken with the idea that I was lost. I was terrified that the ground might open up and swallow me whole. I couldn't hear Amanda. Where had she gone? I couldn't hear anyone. I was afraid she had left me. I cried out, "Amanda, Amanda," but she was right there all the time.

I told her I wanted to go back to our room because I had an awful headache. I wasn't very nice about it.

As soon as I got to our room I climbed into the bed and, without even bothering to take off my coat and hat, pulled the covers over my head. Amanda said she would be downstairs in the parlor if I needed her. I think she was disappointed in me.

As soon as she was gone, I began to cry into the pillow so no one would hear me. The pillow became soaked with my tears. I wanted to rip the blindfold from my face and call a halt to this horrible game. But, of course, there was no blindfold, and this isn't a game.

I told Bess that everyone at school misses her and wants to come visit when she's home on the weekends. She doesn't want to see anyone right now and I told her there was no hurry, which there isn't.

I didn't say anything about church. Mama thinks now, more than ever, Bess should go. Uncle Ted said Mama had to give her time. I'm glad I didn't have to go — I would have felt like a traitor. Fortunately someone had to stay home with Bess.

Saturday, January 23, 1932

I told everyone how much I dread hearing the rising bell (just one of the many bells at Perkins). It's always so cold in the room at 6:30 that I put my clothes under the bed at night, and in the morning gather them up, scuttle back under the covers, and undress and dress all in one motion.

Next, I rush downstairs to help little Helen Harper get dressed. All of the older girls in the cottage are responsible for helping one of the younger ones get dressed in the morning and get ready for bed at night.

Helen's six.

Then there's chapel at 8:25; classes until 12:30, dinner back at the cottage, more classes until 3:00, supper at 5:30, and in bed by 8:00.

When we go to chapel, we form a double line on one side of the hall, and I can hear the boys shuffling into place on the other side.

Inside chapel, Amanda whispered to me that not speaking to the boys is the number one unbreakable rule at Perkins. Not in chapel, in class, or even when walking to and from our cottages. She said they don't want blinks marrying one another and having blink babies.

After chapel, there's usually a speech by the brand-new director, Mr. Elliott. He welcomed all the new teachers, including Miss Salinger, who is our assistant housemother; announced that there are 270 students attending school this year; and explained all the things he is going to do to make Perkins a nicer place (fixing the walkways, and repainting the locker room walls).

"Why bother," Amanda whispered, "repainting the walls in a place where almost everyone can't see the walls?"

I wish she would stop whispering during chapel. Talking of any kind is absolutely forbidden, and it's going to get us both in trouble one of these days.

Miss Salinger showed me how to tell a nickel from a penny and a dime. A penny is smaller than a nickel and a dime is smaller than either of those, which, of course, I already knew. But a dime has ridged edges while nickels and pennies are smooth.

Someday, she said, when she's rich and has some dollar bills, she'll show me how to fold them and place them in my purse so I can tell which ones are dollars and which ones are other denominations.

Miss Salinger has a particular way of speaking. Each word is spoken distinctly and carefully enunciated, which makes sense because she teaches English and drama.

She lives on the floor below us in the big room in the middle of the hall, and she eats at our table.

When I hear her bracelets jangle, it sounds just like the tiny bell Mama put on my cat Smokey after the accident so I would know when she was around.

Miss Salinger smells like Mama's lilacs.

Mrs. Burton called a meeting so she could talk to everyone about keeping Bradlee looking "clean and shiny" as she put it in her sandpaper voice. (I think she sounds that way because of all the cigarettes she smokes.) You can tell that she was quite displeased because she speaks with her false teeth clenched when something is amiss. (At least, that's what Amanda said.) There are, it seems, four areas that need improvement: dry-mopping the floors; keeping the brass work polished; watering the plants; and most important, making sure our rooms are "all buttoned up" before we come down for breakfast.

Amanda *hates* Mrs. Burton. She especially hates the way she treats Eva.

Eva has to sit at Mrs. Burton's table. Mrs. Burton is teaching her proper table manners and breaking her of her bad habits.

Mrs. Burton is constantly telling Eva to stop rubbing her eyes, rocking like a horse, twirling like a top, eating food with her fingers, and acting like a savage.

Eva isn't allowed to leave until she's eaten everything on her plate, which she almost never does, so she has to sit there all by herself until Mrs. Burton sends someone back to tell her she can get up.

Amanda wants to kill Mrs. Burton but says she has to bide her time because she hasn't come up with a foolproof plan yet.

Eva spends all her free time in our room, even though the others girls are quite nice to her (except for Mary Murphy who isn't nice to anyone). Sometimes she plays solitaire with cards that are marked in the upper right-hand corner. The only time she leaves is to go to class, down to eat, or to her voice lessons with Mrs. Alfredo. Eva sings with the glee club.

I asked Eva what she does up there all by herself (besides solitaire), and she said she makes up stories. I asked her what kind of stories and she said knight-in-shining-armor stories.

Even though Eva is our age, she is in the fifth grade, a grade behind us. She told me she has been blind since birth and has been at Perkins her whole life. "I have eyes," she said, "but there is nothing in them."

Some nights Eva cries in her sleep.

Even though Smokey was a birthday present for both of us, she's really always been Bess's cat. I told Bess how much she misses her: She sleeps in Bess's bed during the week, like she thinks Bess is going to return any second.

I want to tell Bess how much we all miss her. The house seems so empty and quiet with her gone.

Friday, January 29, 1932

It snowed almost every day this week. I hate the snow. When I first felt the flakes on my face I became so agitated I could hardly maintain my composure.

Snow ruins everything. You can't tell if you're on the path or have wandered off on to the grass. Everything sounds muffled, not like it usually does. And even if you know where you're going, it's hard to walk because no matter how well the boys shovel, it's still slippery and they never shovel the path in the same way.

I can't wait for winter to be over.

Not Amanda though. She loves the winter, especially snowball fights. She was the first one out the door when our girls took on the girls from Potter. Amanda's a big help because she can see a little.

Oddly enough, Eva goes, too, sitting on the ground behind her making snowballs just as fast as Amanda can throw them.

Naomi Walker and Caroline Cusack asked me if I wanted to join them ice-skating on the pond. They live on our floor in a room with Margaret Kendall and Frances Meara.

I told them I didn't know how to ice-skate.

They're sweet though, especially Naomi. When she came back from ice-skating, she asked me if I wanted to sit with her in the parlor and listen to music on the Victrola. It was quite cozy, sitting near the warmth of the crackling fire with a blanket wrapped around my legs for even more warmth. I almost fell asleep right then and there.

Now that I am unable to see what anyone looks like, I don't know who is nice and who is mean. Who to trust and who to stay away from. Everyone I knew before the accident has a face but the people I have met since do not. I try to make up faces for the ones I like: Amanda, Eva, Miss Salinger.

Amanda, I think, has a round face, green eyes, puffy cheeks covered with freckles, and long, coal-black hair. Eva is small with fine, red hair, and Miss Salinger is quite pretty.

I can't wait until next Friday when Elin comes

with Uncle Ted to pick me up. Amanda and Eva won't come downstairs to meet Uncle Ted, but Elin is going to come right up to the room, which she can because she's a girl.

Then I can find out if the pictures in my head match what they really look like.

I was almost late for class Thursday because of Helen. Sometimes she gets frustrated and starts flailing about. When that happens, it takes a long time to calm her down and get her dressed. By the time I got back to my room, waited my turn in the hall so I could wash, and made my bed, I was late.

I practically ran all the way to class, petrified that I was going to run smack into a tree that someone had planted that very morning. Fortunately no one had and I got to class just as the morning bell was ringing.

Amanda is fascinated that I have a twin. She wants to know everything about us and what it's like.

I think she was disappointed that we're not exactly alike in every way, which is what most people think about twins. We don't like the same foods or the same people. Elin is outgoing and friendly and I like to be by myself. Except for English, she gets better grades (not because she's smarter but because she's older, although only by twelve minutes).

Amanda was surprised when I told her we don't always love people looking at us as twins. That sometimes we wish people would see us as individuals.

Mama says if we didn't look so alike, she would wonder if we were really twins. She says I'm a "poet and a dreamer" just like Daddy. He wrote poems in little notebooks that he kept inside his jacket pocket. Mama gave me one and I still have it.

Amanda did like the story about the time we were in separate places and got cuts at the same exact time on the same exact part of our legs.

Saturday, January 30, 1932

Eva asked me if I could tell her what blue is like. "You used to see," she said, "so what is it like?"

I asked her what she thought it was like, and she said she knows what some of the colors are like: red is noisy; yellow quiet; orange funny, and black not. But she didn't know about blue.

I wanted to tell her it is like the sky on a clear summer's day but, of course, Eva has never seen the sky. I thought and thought and finally I told her that blue is the color of your dreams just before you wake in the morning.

That seemed to satisfy her.

It's from one of Daddy's poems. One of the poems he wrote for Mama. I know it by heart.

Mr. Elliott showed us a beautiful silk banner that was a gift from the Tokyo School for the Blind. It says FROM YOUR FRIENDS IN JAPAN.

After that, we had a guest. He was a blind whistler and whistled "Indian Love Call." I must admit he could whistle up a storm. Fortunately he whistled up a long enough storm that Mr. Elliott was unable to give his customary lengthy lecture. Amanda calls him "The Watertown Windbag" and says that the deaf-blind kids are lucky because they can't hear his speeches.

This week, everyone is talking about the trip the upper schoolboys took to the state prison in Charlestown. They saw death row and the room where the electric chair is. Some say they saw someone actually being electrocuted but I don't believe it.

I can never relax during the week. I'm forever counting steps, remembering where things are so I don't run into them and wondering when I'm going to walk off the edge of a cliff.

The only time I can relax is when I'm home.

Mama and Uncle Ted are starting to treat me more like they used to, before the accident. Mama no longer jumps up to cut my food and pour my milk, and Uncle Ted has stopped asking me a million times a day if there is anything he can get for me.

Mama let me help her bake a pie and has even re-arranged the kitchen so it's easier for me to find things for myself. She showed me the pantry. The canned stuff: soups, vegetables, and fruits are in alphabetical order on separate shelves. Cereal and things in boxes are in the cabinet next to that.

I know it's hard for them and I do appreciate everything they do, but the truth is I feel much better when I do things for myself even if it's more difficult and takes more time.

*　　*　　*

Mrs. Burton called two meetings this past week to go over rules that "certain people" seem to be forgetting.

She said "certain people" most ominously and I'm glad I am not one of them. The rules didn't seem so important that we had to have a whole meeting: Bathing is required twice a week (no exceptions), and permission is needed if you're going to miss a class, visit someone in another cottage, or leave the grounds. Mrs. Burton said anyone found violating these rules will get a demerit.

Amanda thinks she was talking about Mary Murphy, who, according to Amanda, is always going to Watertown Square without permission. I think, however, that Amanda is a little jealous of Mary Murphy because she's a semi, too.

Amanda is certain that Mary Murphy is the one who took her magnifying glass. Amanda uses her magnifying glass to read sometimes and she is quite put out by its disappearance.

Mary Murphy is kind of an oddball because she lives in Cambridge and her family brings her every morning and picks her up every evening. Everyone says she's very, very rich.

Eva cried in her sleep every night last week.

Sunday, January 31, 1932

Elin said that after church, Brian McManus came up to them and said he wanted to come by so he could apologize. Uncle Ted told him to go away.

I'm so proud of Mama. Usually by Thursday night she's worked herself into a nervous state getting everything ready for Bess. She's constantly worried that we'll leave something on the floor and Bess will trip over it or something will be out of place and she won't know where to find it.

I know Mama does it out of love, but Uncle Ted is right: The less we do for Bess the better.

When Brian McManus came up to us after church just as we were getting in the car, I could see that Uncle Ted was trying to control himself. He told Mama and me to get in the car and we did, but I could still hear him tell Brian he wasn't interested in his apologies and then he said, in a very low voice, something about "rotting in hell."

Friday, February 5, 1932

On the way home yesterday, Uncle Ted wanted to stop at Cronin's and surprise Mama with some of Mrs. Cronin's chocolate chip cookies. Mama loves all chocolate chip cookies (as I do), but she especially loves Mrs. Cronin's.

I asked Uncle Ted if I could wait in the car, but he said he was sure Mrs. Cronin would be delighted to "have you visit." That's something I've been noticing recently. People don't like to say "see" if you're blind. That's why Uncle Ted didn't just say that Mrs. Cronin would be delighted to "see" me.

Mrs. Cronin gave me a big greeting, just like always, and the store felt warm and familiar, the smell of cookie dough floating in the air.

I wondered if anyone was there besides Mrs. Cronin. Was Jimmy Bremmer there and did he still want to flirt with me? Were any customers I knew there? I tried to hear but I couldn't because Uncle Ted and Mrs. Cronin were talking too loudly.

Were they staring at me? Why didn't they say anything?

That is what I hate most about being blind: not knowing if someone is right there in front of you, looking right at you.

It's the worst feeling.

I'm embarrassed to say I made Uncle Ted leave before he could even get Mama's cookies. I just couldn't help it.

I was so surprised when Elin told me what Amanda and Eva look like. They are both so different than I imagined.

Eva is not short and doesn't have red hair. Elin said she's tall and quite regal-looking. Amanda was an even bigger surprise. She's really, really little and has close-cropped honey-red hair.

Saturday, February 6, 1932

Mr. Elliott actually told a funny story in chapel. Everyone was so surprised they were unable to laugh. It was called the "Tale of Mr. Wen and Mr. Chen."

A Chinese farmer named Mr. Chen wanted to buy a horse from his neighbor, Mr. Wen.

When Mr. Chen inquired about the horse's availability and condition, Mr. Wen said, "The horse no look good but pull plenty."

Since Mr. Chen wasn't interested in how the horse looked but was interested in how much weight he could pull, he agreed to Mr. Wen's price.

When the horse arrived, Mr. Chen discovered, much to his shock, that it was totally blind! Outraged and believing he had been duped, he sued Mr. Wen.

At the trial, the first thing the judge did was ask Mr. Wen if he knew the horse was blind when he sold it to Mr. Chen.

Mr. Wen admitted that he did know the horse was blind, surprising everyone in the packed courtroom. The judge, who was just as surprised as everyone else, asked, "Why didn't you tell Mr. Chen?" Mr. Wen replied that he did. He had told him repeatedly, "the horse no look good."

With that, the judge dismissed the case.

My favorite classes are Geography, Drama, English, and Gym.

We study Geography much differently than we did at Arlington. We use wooden maps that can be taken apart like jigsaw puzzles. Right now, we're studying the United States and there's a piece for each of the forty-eight states and yarn for the borders. There's also a big, big globe where you can feel the mountains and the elevations of the countries.

My very favorite subjects are English and Drama and not just because Miss Salinger is the teacher, which is what Amanda likes to think.

The gym seems like it's as big as at Arlington and there's a pool, which we didn't have.

I like swimming. There's nothing you have to see and nothing to watch out for. Amanda told me that Mr. Collier, the swimming instructor, has all the furniture in his apartment screwed to the floor so no one can move anything without him knowing.

My two least favorite subjects are Science and Braille.

I don't mind Science when we work with the stuffed animals or take apart those big, fake flowers (although seeing how flowers reproduce isn't exactly my cup of tea), but next week is what I'm truly dreading. We're going to dissect a frog! Right in class! I'm definitely not looking forward to that.

And Mr. Whalen, the Science teacher, makes it ten times worse. He's so strict. Everyone has to face forward in their seats and no "wriggling around" as he calls it.

On the other hand, Braille would be a whole lot worse if it weren't for Mr. Allen. He says I have to be patient because when you lose your sight at the age I did, it takes longer than if you were blind from birth like Amanda and Eva.

Eva says she was given too much silver nitrate by a nurse in the hospital when she was a newborn. And Amanda had the misfortune to have glaucoma. She had four operations, and they did manage to save some of her sight. She has to use eyedrops every day to help relieve the pressure on her eyes.

I thought Mr. Allen was going to say something about Rome not being built in a day, but much to my relief, he didn't.

The only thing I like about Braille is the story of poor Louis Braille who invented the whole thing. The reason I say "poor" is that Louis blinded himself with one of his father's tools. I prefer to have someone like Brian McManus to blame for my fate.

Braille sounds very nice and poetic when Mr. Allen talks about it. He says that Louis's system is simple and elegant because all six dots fit under the tip of your fingers so you can have, as Mr. Allen puts it, the world at your fingertips.

There are six dots: two columns, three dots in each column. C, for instance, is the top dot on the left and right columns; A is the top dot on the left column; and T is the top dot on the left column, the two middle dots, and the bottom dot of the left column, so that C-A-T looks like this: C A T

These six dots can be combined to make all the letters of the alphabet, the punctuation marks, and even musical and mathematical signs.

Unfortunately it's impossible to learn and incredibly tedious to do. I don't think I will ever be able to read and write that way, even though Amanda assures me that everyone has trouble at first.

Mr. Allen, as nice as he is to me, is very stern with

Amanda. I must say, however, she brings it on herself. Last week he scolded her for peeking. Mr. Allen wants Amanda to do her Braille without using her vision, in case something should ever happen — a thought that absolutely horrifies Amanda.

He told her if she peeks again he will put a cloth over her head so she can't see. Frankly, I think Amanda would adore having a cloth put over her head during class.

Saturday, February 13, 1932

Yesterday was Lincoln's birthday, so each student at Perkins received a dollar bill, thanks to Mr. Blaisdell who was a pupil at Perkins many, many years ago. He was very poor at the time and his greatest wish was to have his own spending money, which he never did.

After he graduated he made lots and lots of money selling musical instruments, and when he died he left a great deal of it to Perkins, stipulating that a dollar should be paid to each and every student on Lincoln's birthday. He did this so that all of us could know the thrill of having some money of our own at least once a year.

Amanda, Eva, and I headed right for the canteen.

Amanda showed me how to pour milk without spilling any. You put your hand around the glass and your pointer finger over the rim. Then, when you feel the liquid, you stop. She also said I should keep my food in the center of the plate because it's easier to know where it is that way. If I continue to make good progress she's promised to show me how to strike a match without burning my fingers.

Amanda went on a sleigh ride with everyone else. A rich lady in Boston is providing the sleigh, which Amanda says is so big it has four horses and two drivers. There are even robes and straw to keep you warm.

The cottage was quieter than it's ever been before.

We played one of my favorite games in Gym class last week. It's the one where you stand in line and pass a basketball in front of you till the last girl has it and then she runs around the back to the beginning of the line. There were three teams, ten on each team, and the team who goes through all the girls first, wins. We won.

After that, I tried to jump rope but I can never guess when the rope is coming over my head or heading for my feet. I'm most afraid of running. Miss Morgan explained what you have to do. You either listen for the other runners' footsteps or the sound of the bells everyone wears on their arms. I'm definitely not ready for that.

Miss Morgan said that since I was on the gymnastics team at my old school — Amanda said she probably read my transcript — maybe I would be interested in doing that at Perkins.

I must admit they have all the apparatuses: uneven and parallel bars, flying rings, knotted ropes, and a vaulting board. They even have a trapeze. After the accident, I was convinced there were many things I would never be able to do again and gymnastics was at the top of my list. Right below riding my bicycle.

But maybe I was wrong.

We didn't have to dissect frogs after all. There was some problem with the delivery of the poor things, thank the Lord.

Instead, we are learning all the parts of the cell: the cell wall, the cell membrane, the cytoplasm, the nuclear wall, ribosomes, and Golgi bodies. Elin is helping me study for next week's quiz. Golgi bodies make us both laugh because they sound so friendly and cute.

This afternoon we played musical chairs. Being blind doesn't really make anything more fun but it does make for a pretty funny game of musical chairs. Mary Murphy won but that's because she's a semi.

After musical chairs, I played house with Helen who has lots of rag dolls that her mother makes and sends to her "each and every month" as Helen proudly tells everyone.

We pretend that they are our family. Helen insists on being the mother every single time, and I'm the father who's always late for dinner, which Helen "has slaved over all day." We have three children, all boys, and a dog named Mr. Barker, which is one of Helen's many invented names.

I felt bad because I was rushing that day and I put her shoes on the wrong feet and by nighttime her feet hurt terribly. I promised I would be more careful the next time, but it's hard to tell which shoe is left and which is right when they're so little and you're in such a hurry.

She said she would forgive me if I told her my favorite fairy tale, which I did. Helen was asleep before I even got to the part about the ball.

Although she can be quite frustrating at times, Helen is a sweet girl.

On Wednesday, I banged into a half-open door and cut my forehead so badly I had to go to the infirmary. Mama was distressed about it all weekend, even though I assured her it was little more than a scratch. I didn't want her to know that I needed four stitches.

She said that maybe I should slow down. "Rome wasn't built in a day," she said. Maybe Mama is right, but if I slow down I'm afraid I'll lose the little confidence I have. I think it's better to take my lumps.

Amanda found her magnifying glass. It was in her skirt pocket, which is where it almost always is.

Mr. Elliott talked about Mr. Howe, the founder of Perkins, and the history of blind people. It was a long and pretty boring speech except for one part. That was about Japan a thousand years ago when the government paid blind people to listen to stories of the past and then, when they got older, pass those stories on to younger blind people. They were a kind of living library.

Mr. Howe sounds like an interesting man. He wanted blind people to stop begging on street corners and become useful members of society.

"Obstacles are things to be overcome" was Mr. Howe's motto.

His most famous student was Laura Bridgman, who became deaf and blind when she was three and had scarlet fever.

There are only five deaf-blind students in the whole school and it is difficult to communicate with them because they can't see you or hear you. If they want to know what you are saying they have to hold their fingers up to your mouth, which is the oddest sensation. And if you want to talk to them you have to use the manual alphabet, which I don't even know.

One of the girls in our cottage is deaf and blind.

She is very difficult to handle and appears to be having a temper tantrum twenty-four hours a day. She had spinal meningitis as an infant and lost her sight and hearing at the same time. I just can't imagine that. Amanda said she's calmer now than when she first came to Perkins. She used to crawl backwards everywhere she went because she was so terrified of hitting her poor head yet again.

The year 1932 is the Perkins School for the Blind's hundredth birthday. Amanda whispered that it used to be called The Perkins Asylum for the Blind, like an insane asylum. There's going to be a big centennial celebration at the end of the year.

At first, I thought Amanda only whispered when we were in chapel. But now I realize she does it everywhere, except our room.

I asked her why she whispers all the time, and she said because in a place like Perkins *everyone* can hear a pin drop.

Mary Murphy was late again for breakfast. That's twice this past week because she spends so much time fixing her precious hair. I never saw someone worry so much about how they look.

*　　*　　*

We have to write a paper on the hero or heroine we admire most in history. Eva is doing hers on George Washington because he was the father of our country. You can tell by the way she says it that she doesn't really know what that means.

I'm doing mine on Joan of Arc, and Amanda is doing hers on Franklin Roosevelt, the man who is running for president.

Uncle Ted will be very pleased when he hears that Mr. Roosevelt is Amanda's choice. He wants him to be the next president because he'll do something about the nation's economic plight.

Uncle Ted doesn't like President Hoover, which he mispronounces purposely as "whoever." He says President Whoever is like an ostrich who puts his head in the sand so he doesn't have to face up to the truth.

Uncle Ted was particularly upset this week because he had to lay off more men. He has done everything he possibly can to avoid it, even lowering his own wages. But it wasn't enough.

Mama said that Mrs. Halperin's husband lost his

job and put their car up on blocks because they can't afford the gas.

The country's economic problems are hurting the people at Perkins, too. Some former students who have learned to tune pianos as a trade have lost their jobs because no one can afford to buy a piano these days.

Elin reminded me that Kathleen and Lucy still want to come over and say hello but I think I'd rather they didn't, not right now, anyway.

My sister has learned so much in the past few weeks, much of it because of Amanda, who is just an angel.

I can't believe Bess is considering gymnastics. It was so important to her at Arlington and then the accident happened. She said it made her nervous just to touch the pommel horse and the balance beam.

I wish Mama hadn't gotten so upset about Bess's cut. Mama wanted to call the school and ask them why they weren't taking better care of her baby, but fortunately Uncle Ted was able to calm her down.

Every time I mention that some of the kids want to come over, Bess puts me off. She doesn't even want to talk about it. I don't know what to do. I don't know if I should try and make her see them or leave her alone. Uncle Ted thinks I should let it be, so that's what I'll do.

Lucy is the only one I can really talk to about how odd it is being in school without my sister.

Sunday, February 14, 1932

Mrs. Burton called another meeting this week. This time she wanted to talk to us about table manners, posture, and, of all things, smiling.

Table manners, Mrs. Burton says, are very important because it is one of the things that people use to make judgments about you. Then she declared this Perfect Posture Week, although she didn't explain precisely what that meant.

She said that if we could see how bad our posture is we would be embarrassed, which was a cruel thing to say.

But most of the time she talked about smiling.

Those without sight (Mrs. Burton never, ever says the word "blind") often forget to smile, which is most unfortunate, according to Mrs. Burton. She went on to explain that when we're smiling on the outside it means we're smiling on the inside, whatever that means.

Amanda whispered that the reason Mrs. Burton smiles so much is that she likes to show off her false teeth, which caused Eva to have a laughing fit. Amanda said she's going to steal them. She's going to sneak into Mrs. Burton's room late at night, take them, and leave a note saying, "Let's see how much smiling you do now." That's what she likes best about writing in Braille. No one can tell if it's your handwriting because there is no handwriting.

The most exciting thing that happened all week was going to the canteen with Amanda. The canteen is run by the upper school students.

While we were there, two girls got into an argument about who could eat the most potato chips in sixty seconds.

They bought every bag of chips they had at the canteen and divided them up evenly and then someone said, "On your mark, get set, go!" After much ripping, tearing, munching, crunching, and eventually choking, a winner was declared.

The girl who was doing all the choking was the loser and she ran out of the room knocking over an incredible number of chairs on the way.

It's not really a good idea to run out of a room filled with tables and chairs if you're blind.

Eva had one of her bad dreams Wednesday night. She was sobbing for the longest time.

For all of Bess's good fortune having Amanda and Eva as roommates, it is more than made up for in having Mrs. Burton as a housemother.

Bess agreed with me that Mrs. Burton sounds just like Miss Maly. I told her that as soon as I got to school Monday I was going to tell Miss Maly about Perfect Posture Week — I'm sure she will institute it immediately.

But there's one big difference between the two. Miss Maly may be the strictest teacher at Arlington, but she's not mean. Mrs. Burton's mean as a March snowstorm, as Mama likes to say.

Bess is worried about Eva. She said Eva's dreams are really, really bad and she doesn't know what to do for her.

Friday, February 19, 1932

There's going to be an open house next week. They're expecting more than five hundred visitors: teachers, business leaders, politicians, and other prominent people.

Mr. Elliott said that the open house will introduce the people of the community to all the wonderful things we do at Perkins. ("Like keep the blinks off the streets," Amanda whispered.)

The place has been a beehive of activity. Upper schoolboys are constructing miniature windmills that actually work; the girls are going to read original poems, weave on the handloom, and sew on the sewing machines. The boys in the manual training department will display the baskets and belts they make and the chairs they cane.

"Feeding Time at the Zoo," Amanda calls it. She says people just come to gawk at the blinks doing tricks for their benefit, like monkeys at the zoo.

She said the only thing good about it is seeing just how stupid their questions will be. Last year someone from the Boston Ladies Committee for the Blind asked how the blind students were able to find their mouths when they ate. One of the upper schoolboys said he had magnets put in his teeth that guided the utensil into the "proper orifice."

A man said he noticed that the boys often shoveled snow and he was wondering how they knew when their shovels were full and the boys said, "by smell," and tried not to laugh.

Amanda wants to write a column for *The Goat*. That's the monthly student magazine. It's called that because, supposedly, goats, like blind people, persevere no matter how many obstacles they butt into. There's going to be a Braille edition and a regular text edition.

The column will be called "Ask Alice Adams" (that's Amanda's new pen name). Girls will write to her anonymously about their problems and Amanda (I mean Alice) will answer the most interesting ones.

There are all kinds of other columns: poems, stories, book reports, a "My Most Embarrassing Moment" column, and one on travel where you can tell about interesting places you have visited.

I personally have never been anyplace interesting —

I've never even been outside the state of Massachusetts. But some girls, apparently, have been to all sorts of fascinating places.

One girl travels by train every Christmas to Los Angeles, California! She sees loads of movie stars, especially in Beverly Hills, where the really, really rich people live. She says that Los Angeles is unlike anyplace else on earth. There are palm trees all over, it's seventy degrees even in December, and it never, ever snows. I can't imagine a better place to live.

Saturday, February 20, 1932

Amanda wants to teach me Morse code so we can still communicate even while Mr. Elliott is talking. Despite incessant pressure for her, I have steadfastly refused. I have my hands full, literally, trying to learn Braille, and it is simply impossible for me to even consider learning Morse code at the same time.

I'm glad I'm not a boy. If you're a boy at Perkins you have to take poultry-raising courses. Yuck. I hate chickens. They have a whole flock of hens they have to feed, clean, and care for, including going into their coops and collecting the eggs.

Then they go into Watertown and sell the eggs door-to-door.

We had some really, really, boring talks this week. Mr. Elliott apologized for the noise coming from the basement of the Howe building. He explained that they are installing a new sprinkler system so there won't be a fire like last year. What an incredibly frightening thought.

Someone who used to go to Perkins about a thousand years ago spoke about the history of the petroleum industry.

Mr. Elliott ended with a speech about how Mr. Roosevelt should be an inspiration to all of us because he has had to battle against terrible odds on account of his being paralyzed with infantile paralysis.

I don't think being crippled is quite the same thing as being blind. I can imagine someone who is crippled becoming president of the United States, but not someone who is blind.

Miss Salinger does so many things that mean a lot.

She always says hello as soon as she comes into a room and good-bye when she leaves. That may seem insignificant but it's not if you're blind.

I'm consistently unnerved when I discover that there is someone in the room with me and I didn't know.

She has offered to record my diary entries during the week!

She was talking in class about her own diary and after class I told her how I used to keep my diary every single day but now I can only do it on weekends because Elin has to help me.

I was embarrassed because I wouldn't want her to think I was telling her that so she would offer to help. But she assured me it was no trouble and we agreed to devote an hour every Wednesday evening as "Diary Time."

Uncle Ted had to take me back to school early so I could get ready for our visit with the director. Every Sunday afternoon, he meets with one of the cottages and this Sunday it's our turn.

Someone has taken Mrs. Burton's false teeth! She didn't say anything about it herself, but Amanda says

Mrs. Burton hardly opened her mouth all week and ate only mashed potatoes. She didn't yell at Eva even once, which is most extraordinary.

Amanda says she didn't take them, but I'm not sure I believe her.

Wednesday night I had a bad dream about the accident. I was sledding smoothly down the snow-covered hill, the cold wind whipping against my face. Then, out of the corner of my eye I saw Brian McManus. That idiotic grin of his looked even bigger than usual.

Then I realized it was bigger because he was about to crash into me and that's where the dream was so different from the real thing.

Unlike when it actually happened, in the dream I knew that Brian McManus's idiot grin would be the last thing I would ever see and there was nothing I could do about it.

I think Bess was concerned that I would be jealous that Miss Salinger is going to be recording her diary during the week. It was very sweet of her to be so considerate of my feelings but, as I told her, I thought it was the most marvelous news.

For one thing, it will help ease the burden on us during the

*weekends when we have to record all that went on during the week,
which is quite a lot. Not only that, it will make Mama happy. Just
last week she said, once again, that she hardly gets to see Bess when
she's home because we spend so much time in her room.*

*Bess still doesn't want anyone to visit, not even Lucy. I've never
seen her like this. Usually Bess is so reasonable about everything.
But not this. This is a closed book.*

Wednesday, February 24, 1932

Mr. Elliott has the funniest furniture. There are ani-
mal heads carved into the ends of the chair arms. I
think mine had a lion or a tiger. Amanda says she is
sure hers was a bear chair.

His house is right on the grounds. It smelled of cig-
arette smoke and shaving lotion. The refreshments he
served weren't very refreshing: warm grape juice and
tasteless cookies with little cherry halves on top.
Amanda says the cherry halves were green, but I'm
not sure if I should believe her.

Mrs. Burton said we should think of nice questions
to ask the director and warned us that we'd better be on

our best behavior. "Wear your Sunday manners" was how she put it.

Much to her displeasure, however, most of the questions were really, really silly. Mary Murphy asked if the water in the pool could be made warmer — and that was one of the better ones.

Saturday, February 27, 1932

Amanda thinks she's figured out how to kill Mrs. Burton. She's going to invite her to an ice-skating party on the pond. Before she gets there, Amanda's going to carve out a big circle in the ice so that when Mrs. Burton steps on it she'll sink right to the bottom and it will be bye-bye Mrs. Burton.

Frankly I think there are more holes in this plan than the ones in the ice and Amanda's head.

For one thing, I can't imagine Mrs. Burton ice-skating, let alone attending an ice-skating party on a frozen pond. And even if by some odd chance she did, wouldn't she be a little suspicious that she was the only one there?

Now Amanda is mad at me because I didn't think too much of her plan.

The one thing that bothers me about Perkins is that you're never alone — it's almost impossible. You're always doing something with someone and someone's always in your room or you're in theirs. That's the part I miss most — having my own room.

People I like smell nice and people I don't, don't. I never noticed that before. Uncle Ted smells like pipe tobacco and Mama like the kitchen. Mrs. Burton smells like mothballs and Mr. Whalen like a chemical factory. Amanda doesn't really smell like anything because she spends half her life in the bathtub.

The upper schoolboys' wrestling team has gone to Philadelphia to compete against Overbrook, which is a blind school, too. Next week the boys from Overbrook are coming here for a swim meet.

I've been practicing my gymnastics. I'm surprised that you don't need to see as much as I thought you did.

Miss Morgan says I should go slow. "Rome wasn't

built in a day," she said, or at least that's what I think she said. It's hard to hear her sometimes because she's always chewing gum.

Daddy used to say that. "Rome wasn't built in a day." So does Uncle Ted. And Mama. I wonder why adults always say the same things.

I finished my report on Joan of Arc. The most amazing thing I learned about her wasn't how she single-handedly saved her country but that she couldn't even read or write.

I wonder, what would it be like to hear the voice of God?

Of course, Amanda had to make fun of the report. She says she, too, hears voices and that the voices are saying over and over, "Kill Mrs. Burton. Kill Mrs. Burton."

Saturday, March 5, 1932

We stayed up late last night hoping to hear news about the Lindbergh baby.

The man on the radio called the kidnapping a "national disgrace." He said if criminals can "snatch" the son of America's greatest hero, no one in the country is safe.

Uncle Ted says it just shows how desperate people have become. He has been glued to the radio ever since it happened. Mama said he had it on so much it was going to start a fire. Uncle Ted told Mama she should stick to things she knows about, like cooking.

The night before the kidnapping, we had our own unsolved mystery. It was discovered that someone had taken all the telephone change from the iron box in the parlor. If you want to make a telephone call, you just put in your nickel and if you need change you take it. It's all on the honor system but clearly someone in the cottage is not honorable.

Mrs. Burton is furious. She said that theft has no place at Perkins and especially not at Bradlee Cottage. She has consulted with the director and they have decided to give the thief twenty-four hours to return "their ill-gotten gains."

Amanda's sure Mary Murphy took the money because she spent this whole past week in the canteen, which is surely an exaggeration, let alone proof of anything. Amanda said she was buying candy for everyone and acting like someone who "had robbed a bank." Those were Amanda's very words.

Amanda's going to follow Mary every minute to see if she puts back the money into the iron box.

I'm doing much better at dinner, especially in the milk pouring area. Sometimes I don't even have to put my finger in the glass because I can *hear* when it's getting full. I can butter my own bread and am much better at finding where my food is on the plate.

All anyone in school talks about is the Lindbergh kidnapping — even the teachers. Everyone's frightened to go to sleep at night. There are bulletins constantly and the police are searching night and day. Mama says there is a coast-to-coast dragnet. Colleen told me that her family was stopped by the police on Beacon Hill and questioned because her baby brother has blond, curly hair and blue eyes just like the Lindbergh baby.

Lucy says you don't have to worry unless you're rich. The kidnappers only take kids who come from rich families. The trouble is I'm not sure if we're rich or not. I know we're not poor.

Uncle Ted says we're luckier than most because we still have our house, the car, and food on the table.

He says the Lindbergh kidnapping would never have happened if it wasn't for the bad times. People feel helpless and they are tired of begging for jobs or going on relief. They think rich people don't care about their troubles and they're gambling on six-day bicycle races, 4,000-mile roller derbies, pie-eating contests, and dance marathons. Things have gotten so out of control they're starting to rob banks and steal children to make money.

Uncle Ted says somebody better do something soon or else the whole thing's going to come unglued.

I never heard Uncle Ted talk like this before.

Mama says he's frustrated because of all the trouble at work and what happened yesterday with Mrs. Francis, his secretary.

Mr. Francis lost his job last month. They had to pawn most of their furniture and he is shining shoes in the streets to help make ends meet. Mrs. Francis asked to see Uncle Ted. But as soon as she sat down in his office, she started crying and couldn't stop long enough to tell Uncle Ted what was on her mind.

Uncle Ted suggested that they talk later in the day but Mrs. Francis went home early, saying she had a terrible headache.

He told us he was going to lend her some money, just to tide them over.

Wednesday, March 9, 1932

I hate Braille.

I don't know what's worse, learning to write it or learning to read it.

Writing Braille is an excruciatingly tedious process. You have to put your paper in between your Braille slate, which is a two-piece metal frame. Like a sandwich. The Braille slate has row after row of little windows and even littler coves inside each window, which is where you place your stylus. The stylus looks like a miniature ice pick only it's blunt and has a knobby top that you grasp in your palm and push down on to make the raised dots on the paper.

If you don't make sure the stylus is precisely where you want it before you push down, you'll have no idea what you're writing.

It takes hours just to punch one sentence.

And that's not all!

You have to write from right to left because the raised dots come out on the other side of the paper (which is where you actually do the reading). You can't see where the dot is unless you take the paper out of the frame and turn it over, which is just too much trouble, if you ask me.

Sometimes I make mistakes and try to rub out the dot with my fingers, which doesn't work very well.

And reading Braille is just as hard.

Because I'm a beginner I'm working with the dots that are bigger than the regular ones. Even with the big dots, I can't tell one letter from another. I'll never be able to read the teeny, tiny dots Amanda and Eva are reading. They're simply too small and too close together and no matter how many times I go over them I can't tell them apart.

Amanda says I should put Vaseline on my hands and sleep with gloves on. That will soften my fingers and make them more sensitive. Maybe so, but I have enough to do getting ready for bed each night without adding Vaseline and gloves to my list.

Saturday, March 12, 1932

The Donnellys came over for dinner last night. Mr. Donnelly is the president of the bank and now that

Uncle Ted has taken over Daddy's company he, too, has to have them over at least once a year.

I used to think the thing I hated most about Mr. Donnelly was the way he looked: his fat, florid face with those fleshy chipmunk cheeks and that smug smile.

Now I know that what he thinks is even worse than the way he looks.

As usual, he had too much to drink (Mrs. Donnelly tries to make him stop but he never pays her any mind), and he went on and on about who's to blame for the country's economic woes.

According to Mr. Donnelly, it's all because of the immigrants who are "flooding" into the country. He said we would be better off if we didn't let any of them in because most of them are on relief, which is just what they deserve.

Uncle Ted was sitting next to me and I could hear him shifting around in his chair as if he was trying to find a comfortable place to wait out the storm. When he wasn't fidgeting he was puffing away furiously on his pipe.

Uncle Ted is pretty quiet, but finally he had heard enough. He told Mr. Donnelly that he didn't know half as much about people as he thought he did. I never heard Uncle Ted sound that angry before.

He asked Mr. Donnelly if he had seen the families lined up at the soup kitchens, or the poor souls who sleep on park benches wrapped in old newspapers that they hope will protect them from the icy winter winds, or the grown men fighting each other for scraps left in garbage cans. He asked if Mr. Donnelly had seen the hundreds of huts that entire families are forced to live in. Huts made from packing crates covered with flattened tin cans. So many, they are now filling up vacant lots that have been transformed into teeming shantytowns.

Uncle Ted asked him if he had talked to any of these men who are getting "what they deserve." Without waiting for him to answer, he told him about Mr. Kelliher who spends his nights crying because he can't feed his family, and Mr. Jackson who lost his job and was caught stealing a loaf of bread, which landed him in jail and now his family's worse off than ever before.

Mr. Donnelly and Mrs. Donnelly got up to leave but Uncle Ted followed them to the door, talking all the while.

It was a shame, Uncle Ted said, that he couldn't talk to Mr. Watkins. Surely he knew Mr. Watkins because yesterday morning Mr. Donnelly's bank notified Mr. Watkins that they were repossessing his house because he had failed to meet his mortgage payment. But he couldn't talk to Mr. Watkins because Mr. Watkins had decided that, rather than face his wife and five children, he would check into a hotel room and blow his brains out with a shotgun.

The sound of Mr. Donnelly slamming the front door gave me a scare because it sounded, for a moment, like what a shotgun must sound like.

The house was still and Mama asked Elin and I to help her clear the dishes and Uncle Ted went up to his room.

Wednesday, March 16, 1932

Being left-handed makes reading Braille even harder. You have to read with your right hand while your left stays at the beginning of the line. That's to let you know where you started so that when your right hand finishes a line it can return to where your left hand is and then move down to the next line.

Mr. Allen said eventually I'll be reading so fast I won't even use my left hand because it will slow my right hand down. I asked Amanda and Eva about this and they said they never used their left hands, but I can't imagine that ever being the case for me.

The problem is I miss reading terribly. Before the accident I used to read all the time and now I read nothing. Without books you spend too much time thinking about small, foolish things.

Elin asked if I am homesick when I am away at Perkins. She sounds so sad lately. I told her I miss everyone, especially her, which is true. But it's also true that I'm so busy all day I don't really have time to be homesick.

When I first knew I was going to Perkins I was worried that blind kids wouldn't be as smart, pretty, or nice as my friends at Arlington. I was so relieved to find that it wasn't that way at all. But I don't tell Elin how much easier Amanda and Eva have made it for me because then she might think I don't need her any-more, which isn't true at all. No one can ever, ever re-place my sister, no matter what. I wanted to tell her that. I know she feels bad that we are apart — she always takes things to heart more than I do. But, somehow, I just couldn't find the words.

Miss Morgan said we should remember that team-work and sportsmanship are the most important things about Friday's inter-cottage competition. I wish I could agree with her, but I honestly think the most important thing is winning the trophy.

I know I shouldn't have asked Bess if she was homesick. And maybe I should have said something about reading her Wednesday-night entries. I can tell she knows I read them. I just couldn't help it.

Bess seems so content at Perkins. Sometimes I wonder if she misses me as much as I miss her.

Of course Bess has always been the self-sufficient one. More than anyone else I know, Bess gets along fine on her own. I guess that's turned out to be a good thing.

When she said I sounded sad I told her it was because of what happened at school Thursday. It was at least half true because it did make me sad.

David Pollard was crying and Mr. Armstrong called him up to his desk. Even though they were talking really low, I could still make out what they were saying because I can lip-read. Mr. Armstrong wanted to know what was the matter. At first, David didn't want to say anything but finally Mr. Armstrong got it out of him. He said he was crying because he was hungry. That he didn't have any dinner last night or the night before and he had nothing for breakfast.

Mr. Armstrong told us to read and remain quiet till he returned and took David to the principal's office. I didn't see David for the rest of the day or on Friday.

Saturday, March 19, 1932

I was so excited when we entered the gym. Amanda and Mary Murphy held the Bradlee banner and we all wore our cottage colors.

I spent hours getting my hair to look nice. Finally we (meaning Amanda) decided it would look best in a bun. I'd never worn it in that way before. Amanda put a little lipstick on me and she said I looked beautiful and I told her I would have to take her word for it.

We didn't win the prize for best cottage song, even though Eva sang a solo that was so glorious not another sound was made the whole time she was singing.

It was such an exciting day. Mama, Uncle Ted, and Elin came. So did Miss Salinger's brother and many of the parents.

We won the relay race but lost the basketball game 32–9. I ran the anchor leg of the relay and almost bumped into someone but fortunately heard the bell on her arm just in time.

If I had been playing we would have won the basketball game (or certainly not lost as badly as we did). Unfortunately only upper schoolgirls play basketball. They have a bell tied to the basket so that you know when you've scored.

We lost the sack race to Glover cottage pretty badly, too. I must admit with the exception of Naomi Walker, the Bradlee girls are not blessed with great athletic ability. We did manage to win the tug-of-war, however.

Afterwards, we all went to the playground and played on the seesaw and the jungle gym. Then we decided to see how many of us could pile into the rocking boat (fourteen) and how long we could swing without stopping (fifty-two minutes). We could have gone even longer but Caroline Cusack said she was getting sick, which turned out to be true.

I told Miss Salinger that I don't want to learn Braille, that I prefer to write square hand. But she said it is better to learn Braille because no matter how good I became at square hand, my penmanship will eventually deteriorate. "Square hand," she said, "is good for signing your name and things like that but Braille is better in the long run."

She said I should be patient and remember that Rome wasn't built in a day.

Wednesday, March 23, 1932

Over the weekend, Elin said I don't talk as much as I used to. She's probably right, and I just don't notice it when I'm at Perkins.

I have gotten quiet since the accident. I have to

hear as much as I can so I don't speak. Maybe that's why Eva says so little.

I asked Elin if she is bored now because I don't talk so much. She said she is enjoying being the one who does most of the talking for a change.

I could tell that she had something on her mind and wished she would just say it. Finally, she did.

"What's it like?" she said. "Tell me the truth."

I told her about the night I first truly realized what had happened to me. That there was no hope. That no doctor and no operation was going to give me back my sight. I was blind and that was that.

That night everything changed. Everything.

I was terrified. I couldn't imagine not seeing ever again. I didn't understand what I had done to deserve such a terrible fate. Things I hadn't given any thought to now took an enormous amount of time and effort: getting dressed, eating, combing my hair. Everything.

I decided I wouldn't go anywhere, wouldn't do anything, wouldn't see anyone. I would wear the same thing every day; even better, I would wear only black. Black blouses, black sweaters, black skirts. That way I wouldn't have to worry about not being properly color-coordinated. Besides, I was in mourning, wasn't I? Mourning for my lost sight.

Then came Perkins.

And suddenly I had no choice. I had to learn to find my way down the hall to the bathroom, how to get to the Howe building, how to eat, get dressed, make my bed, and clean my room.

And now, little by little, it's not so bad.

All week long I say to myself, over and over, don't say this to Bess and don't say that to Bess. But then, as soon as she walks in the door I just blurt it right out, like I hadn't even given it a thought.

I'm just furious with myself. As if Bess doesn't have enough to worry about, she has to be concerned with my feelings.

Bess was so sweet about it, which of course I knew she would be. She said maybe she doesn't talk as much as she used to because she doesn't feel like she used to, which made me feel about two inches tall.

I could tell she was feeling really sad talking about Eva. Eva makes her think that maybe, after you're blind for a while, you draw back inside yourself and hardly speak. I said that obviously being blind hasn't affected Amanda's ability to speak, which made us both laugh.

I thought I had convinced myself to never, ever ask her that, but it was expanding inside me like a giant balloon. Each day, it grew bigger and bigger. I was afraid that unless something happened I was going to burst into a million pieces.

Our whole lives we've always known what the other was thinking and there was no way Bess didn't know what was on my mind.

I think she was relieved to talk about it. I hope she was.

Saturday, March 26, 1932

Miracle of miracles! Mr. Donnelly died of a heart attack yesterday! One minute he was sitting at his desk signing some papers and the next minute he was on the floor.

When Elin told me I couldn't wait to talk to Mama and Uncle Ted. But Elin said they were being very solemn and pretending there was nothing funny about it.

Sure enough she was right. When I said something at dinner, all Uncle Ted said was that the Lord works in mysterious ways. Elin said that when he said this she could see just the faintest flicker of a smile on Mama's lips.

Easter vacation is in less than two weeks. I asked Mama if Eva could come and stay with us. I'm sure Amanda will be going to Nantucket so she can be with her family and poor Eva doesn't have anyone. Mama said that would be fine, which I knew it would.

I can't wait to tell Eva the good news!

Last week I decided to try snapping my fingers like Amanda said. I didn't really think anything would happen.

Mostly I just felt foolish, walking down the cavernous corridors of the Howe building, snapping my fingers for no apparent reason. I imagined it would be my misfortune to have Mr. Elliott walk by at that precise moment. I could picture the look on his face as he pondered just how crazy I was.

Much to my surprise, however, after a while the sound did change, just as Amanda said it would. Just slightly, yet it had definitely changed. The echo was shorter, and tighter, like I was in a confined place. I stopped, put my arms out and felt big doors, and realized the sound had changed because I had come upon the library.

*   *   *

I am really proud of Mama. The way she sounded, you would have thought having Eva visit Easter weekend was the most delightful idea she ever heard. Fortunately Bess couldn't see the worry in Mama's eyes.

We are all still getting used to making sure we didn't forget to close a cupboard door, leave something on the floor, or thoughtlessly move a piece of furniture. Now, on top of that, we will have a stranger staying with us who is unfamiliar with everything in the house.

After breakfast, I went for a walk with Uncle Ted. He's right — it means a lot to Bess and we will have to be even more vigilant to ensure that nothing happens to Eva.

Wednesday, March 30, 1932

What a terrible week — and it's only half over!

When I returned to school on Sunday I discovered that Amanda isn't going home for Easter vacation.

A letter came Friday from her mother saying that the fishing business isn't good and they won't be able to come get her this year.

Amanda acted like it was the most matter-of-fact

news in the world but I could tell she was upset from the little quiver in her voice.

I didn't know what to do. I couldn't just leave Amanda behind at Perkins, all by herself, while everyone went home for Easter.

I called Elin.

Elin said she would talk to Mama and called me back in an hour. I just sat there and waited by the phone. Much to my blessed relief Elin said she would sleep in my room and Uncle Ted would move the cot into her room so that Amanda and Eva could sleep there.

Mama said we had no choice — we would just have to pray that everything will turn out right in the end. Bess was so happy she started to cry when I told her it was okay with Mama — Amanda could come, too. I just hope we're doing the right thing.

Wednesday, April 6, 1932

Mama made my favorite Easter dinner: pot roast, mashed potatoes, boiled onions, applesauce, and mince pie with vanilla ice cream.

Everyone had such a good time, I only wish Daddy could have been there.

Elin spent almost all Sunday teaching Eva to whistle, a talent which fascinates Eva and which she has taken to quite readily.

Uncle Ted told the best story — only I'm not so sure it was just a story.

One day a man was driving his truck along a highway in the Southwest and came upon a man buried up to his neck in the ground. The man said a sudden and particularly ferocious dust storm had put him in this predicament. The man who was driving the truck asked if he wanted help getting out and a ride into town. The man said he would appreciate some help getting out but he was on a horse and didn't need a ride.

Amanda laughed so hard I thought she was going to fall off her chair.

The only thing that ruined it was going to church on Easter Sunday.

Mama knew I didn't want to go in the worst way but she wouldn't hear any more about it. I hadn't been to church or seen anyone from school since the accident and Mama was displeased with me.

I wish I had gone before because I thought going with Amanda and Eva was going to make it ten times harder. I couldn't help but feel that everyone was looking at us when we walked in. I pictured them turning around and putting their hands to their mouths and tittering.

I was so nervous that I gripped Amanda's arm tighter with each step down the aisle. I could feel my face getting flushed, and I feared I would faint dead away from embarrassment.

Then I heard someone whistling, someone real close to me. It was Eva. I was furious at her. She knew I was terrified of this moment and here she was whistling like we were talking a walk in the park. I tried not to be distracted, worried that I might stumble and fall, which would be more than mortifying. But the tune was so familiar, I knew I had heard it before, yet I couldn't quite remember what it was.

Dee da da. Dee da da. Dee da da da. Dee da da da.

Then I realized what she was whistling:

Three blind mice.

Three blind mice.
See how they run.
See how they run.
They all ran after the farmer's wife.
She cut off their tails with a carving knife.
Did you ever see such a sight in your life?
As three blind mice.

I started to laugh despite myself and continued until we sat down, stopping only after a most strenuous effort on my part. I was sure that everyone was wondering what I was laughing about but I was too grateful to Eva for relieving the unbearable tension to care.

It made everything better, even after the service when I had to talk to everyone. I could hear in their voices how afraid they were and how much distance had come between us, now that I can no longer see.

Even though that realization saddened me (but didn't surprise me) all I could think about was Eva's performance of "Three Blind Mice" and try not to start laughing again.

I think Mama spoke for the three of us when she said, "Thank the Lord they all returned to school safe and sound." Of course,

Amanda gets along quite well on her own and everyone fell in love with Eva. She is so, so quiet, but somehow mysteriously manages to communicate her sweetness.

Bess said she hasn't seen Eva eat that much the whole time she's been at Perkins. Besides whistling, the only sound she made the entire weekend was saying, "Yes, please" when offered another helping and "Thank you so much for having me, Mrs. Brennan." Eva is such a well-mannered girl.

Unfortunately I can't say quite the same for Amanda. Bess says she can be pretty bossy especially when something is troubling her, like the news from home. But Bess is quick to add that she is a good and true friend. She wouldn't know where she'd be if it weren't for Amanda.

Bess wanted me to help get her out of going to church, but there wasn't anything I could do about it. Mama is generally agreeable to most things but once she puts her foot down about something it stays down.

Saturday, April 9, 1932

April is my favorite month and not just because of my birthday (which is what Amanda thinks). April means winter is over and you can breathe a sigh of relief. The air smells fresh and fragrant and everything begins to bud and bloom. The trees are starting to blossom already and the tulip bulbs Mr. Hadley gave us to plant are finally coming up.

Miss Salinger announced we're going to put on a play in front of the entire lower school. Even more exciting is that the play is written by Miss Salinger herself.

It's called *When Will This Cruel War Be Over?*, and it's about a Southern girl during the Civil War.

Miss Salinger said prima donnas need not apply because this is going to be hard work.

I'm not sure what a prima donna is but I don't think I am one.

I'm actually making progress with my Braille, although Amanda still calls it "snail Braille," which she thinks is hysterical but I don't.

It's taken me three months but I can now identify nearly every single letter in the alphabet. And that's not all: I wrote my first complete sentence in Braille! Actually it's my second complete sentence but the first one that made any sense.

Sunday, April 10, 1932

I hear people differently than I used to. I hear the way their voices go high or low, fast or slow. Some voices are cold and hard and some soft and warm.

Sometimes I have trouble distinguishing individual voices if everyone's talking at once. Uncle Ted is so considerate, he knows I find the radio distracting if we're talking and he turns it off then — even if *Amos and Andy* is on.

Amanda says hearing is better than seeing when it comes to judging people. She thinks you make less mistakes that way because people can fool you too easily if you can see them. A pretty face or a nice smile can hide a lot. But if it's just the sound of their voices, they can't fool you because voices don't lie.

Wednesday, April 13, 1932

I got the part I wanted!

I'm going to play Rachel, who is the main character's slightly cuckoo cousin. Emma (the main character) is a little too nice for my taste. Rachel is more like a real girl, more like me.

When the play opens, Emma's beloved brother has just returned home, dead. Her aunt Caroline and cousin Rachel have arrived to help Emma care for her sick mother. Her father is, of course, off fighting the war.

Rachel is beside herself with agitation about the disastrous course the war has taken and the impending defeat of the South. She fears that the dreaded Yankee soldiers are going to destroy everything she has ever known.

Naomi Walker is playing Emma, so we do our scenes together and they are so much fun. I especially like the ones where we talk about boys and marriage.

Saturday, April 16, 1932

I had the most wonderful birthday.

Mama got me a new dress and Uncle Ted gave me a clock. It has raised dots instead of numbers and no glass so I can feel where the hands are pointing. Elin gave me a bottle of the most glorious bubble bath. I think she really liked my present — a basket I wove for her at Perkins.

Friday morning as soon as I got up, Eva made me go downstairs right away, even before I got dressed or made my bed or anything. Everyone was gathered in the living room and they sang "Happy Birthday" with Eva's angelic soprano soaring high above the other voices.

And little Helen Harper gave me a rag doll that she had her mother make especially for me.

Wednesday, April 20, 1932

I did it!

I can write Braille!

I wrote my first letter to Mama. It said, "I love you," only it came out, "I pove you," because I put an extra dot that made the "l" a "p." Thankfully Mama will not be able to notice.

I've decided to let Amanda cut my hair short like hers. She's right, it's just too much time and too much trouble caring for long hair when you're blind.

We've decided to do it tonight, right before bed.

Saturday, April 23, 1932

I went on my first school trip last week.

We packed a picnic lunch, went to the Boston Gardens, and rode on the swan boats. Eva just *loved* the swan boats. I've never seen her so animated.

She insisted on going with each group, which wasn't exactly fair because she wasn't waiting her turn the way she was supposed to. But someone always let her take their place just because she's Eva.

Mary Murphy managed to find a spider that bit her on the cheek and it swelled up until it was almost as big as the whole rest of her head. She moaned and groaned and didn't stop talking about it all the way home.

Amanda said the reason we go on trips is that they think it's a good idea for us to spend as much time as possible with sighted people. That way we can learn how to act normally and not act like blinks.

Wednesday, April 27, 1932

Even though everyone said nice things about my hair, they seemed quite distressed about it, especially Elin.

Mama said it was flattering, although her voice was saying, "Oh my God, Bess, what have you done?" Uncle Ted said it was quite a change, and Elin said she thought it made me look older, but she didn't say if she thought that was good or bad.

All of us were caught off guard by Bess's hair. Even reliable Uncle Ted was babbling away about it being time for a change or something like that. Mama sounded equally unconvincing and I'm afraid I mumbled something that wasn't quite a lie yet wasn't the truth. I couldn't say the truth. The truth was it was the first time Bess and I didn't look exactly alike and I don't think Bess even thought of it that way.

Saturday, April 30, 1932

I told Elin Amanda's latest idea: that we change places for a week and see if anyone can tell. Elin thought it might be a little difficult for me to take her place without anyone noticing, especially with my new haircut.

We laughed about that and talked about the time Elin took both math classes, hers and mine, because she was so much better than me and we both got A's.

And we talked about how Daddy was the only one who could always tell us apart and then suddenly Elin started to cry. She was crying so hard I couldn't understand what she was saying. I thought she was still upset because I had cut my hair and I tried to assure her that I would let it grow and that it wouldn't take very long but she said that wasn't why she was crying.

"Mirror, mirror on the wall," she said and then the tears started flowing with even more ferocity.

"We're not twins anymore. We're not the same because you can't see and I can."

"Mirror, mirror on the wall," she kept saying over and over, and then we were both crying as I held her in my arms. We must have fallen asleep because the next thing I knew the morning light was warming my face.

Wednesday, May 4, 1932

Eva has been rehearsing her song for the graduation ceremonies for the past two weeks. She's excited and so am I. It's going to be truly wonderful: The boys' choir is going to be singing with her but she's the featured soloist. Amanda said Eva sang last year at the Christmas concert and it was a sensation. There are only twenty students good enough to be in the glee club and Eva is the best of the best.

Her voice sounds musical even when she's just speaking. Every word hits a particular note, like perfect little pearls, and her sentences have a rhythm to them. It's more like she's singing to you than talking to you.

We went to a recital at Dwight Hall Monday night. I didn't really want to go but Eva has been looking forward to this particular performance all year, and I knew she wouldn't go alone, despite her boasts to the contrary.

On the way over, I asked her why she likes to sing so much. She said it's because when she's singing she isn't blind. That singing has nothing to do with seeing and when she sings she doesn't have to go slow, or feel her way, or worry that she's making a fool of herself like she does all the rest of the time.

I enjoyed the recital more than I thought I would because I recognized the music. Daddy used to play it nearly every weekend morning on the Victrola. I heard it so many times I could even hum it by heart.

Eva was impressed that I knew the music well enough to hum along and wanted to know how I knew.

Unfortunately I was unable to answer her. The words just stuck in my throat and my eyes welled up with tears. Sometimes I miss Daddy so much I feel like I'll die if I even think about it.

Graduation day is only five weeks away. Seven students are going to graduate from Perkins and I'll be going into the upper school.

It's all going by so quickly. Although I am looking forward to spending the summer with my family, the thought of being away from Perkins frightens me. At Perkins, I know just where I'm going (at least most of the time). I know my way around the grounds, where all the buildings are, and where the rooms inside the buildings are located. I just feel more comfortable when I'm at Perkins with Amanda, Eva, and the rest of my friends there.

Of course I've learned to get around my own house but everything surrounding it is one vast, uncharted ocean of uncertainty.

Saturday, May 7, 1932

Uncle Ted took Elin, Amanda, and me to the movies this afternoon (Eva couldn't come because she was singing with the glee club at Watertown High School).

He gave each of us a dime so we could pay for ourselves. We had to sit in the first row so Amanda could see.

Grand Hotel was playing and I was able to follow what was happening even though there were lots and lots of characters and everything was happening to all of them at once. I listened carefully to every word so I wouldn't get lost.

It's the first movie I've seen since the accident.

After the movie, we went to the drugstore on Beacon Street and sat in a big booth. Elin and I had strawberry sundaes and Amanda had a whole banana split!

Wednesday, May 11, 1932

Amanda has been imitating Greta Garbo every day since we got back from seeing *Grand Hotel*. She thinks

Greta Garbo's voice is very "exotic," at least that's how she put it. It's been nothing but "dahling" this and "dahling" that and "I vant to be alone" so many times you wish she were.

Saturday, May 14, 1932

Cousin Rachel is such a wonderful character. One of the reasons I like playing her is she's so unlike me in every way, except that we're both pretty.

For one thing, I certainly don't put on airs the way she does and I have every intention of marrying and raising a family of my own, unlike her. Rachel has absolutely no use for boys, all of whom she considers untrustworthy. Although I agree with her in the majority of cases (boys can be quite problematic) there are exceptions.

Billy, for example.

I met Billy last Thursday. It was an absolutely glorious spring day and we were sitting on the wall that runs along the path that leads to our cottage. It's so nice now that the weather is getting warmer and we can sit and talk after class.

There were some boys a little ways down from us. Although Amanda has warned me a number of times that the most important rule at Perkins is never, ever talk to a boy, I was just too curious. Whatever they were doing was making a funny sound like stones colliding in midair and I had to find out what it was.

I sidled down the wall till I could hear them talking and asked what was making that sound.

For the longest time no one answered but then this boy with a voice that sounded like cinnamon and honey said they were playing dice baseball and the sound was the dice they threw.

Amanda, who had decided if I could break a rule so could she, asked if we could play. I thought that was a little *too* bold but that's Amanda, and there's no changing her.

Another boy, not the first boy, said that girls weren't allowed to play. Although we both thought that was utterly ridiculous we left them to their precious game of dice baseball.

The very next day I was sitting in the same exact spot waiting for Amanda and Eva when the first boy, the one with the syrupy voice, asked me if I still wanted to know how to play dice baseball.

I was going to tell him it was Amanda, not me, who wanted to play but his voice was so beckoning I couldn't help but say yes.

And, besides, I was eager to learn how to play.

I like the feel of the dice rattling around in my hand and being able to feel the numbers on the sides so no one has to tell me what is happening.

He told me his name is Billy and that he lives in Tompkins. When I heard that, I asked if the rumor was true. Everyone knows that some of the boys in Tompkins snuck out recently, took the trolley into Boston, and went to see a Red Sox game at Fenway Park.

He said it was true but that I had to promise not to tell anyone he told me. But I did, of course, I couldn't wait to tell Amanda.

I asked him if it was scary sneaking out like that, and he said it was but it was worth it because the Red Sox beat the Yankees 3–2. Billy hates the Yankees.

Wednesday, May 18, 1932

Naomi Walker is gone.

Her father came down Sunday night with no warning, took her from her room, threw her into his car, and drove away with her. Miss Salinger said there was nothing anyone could do. She called Mr. Elliott, who came right away and tried to convince Mr. Walker to reconsider, but he refused.

Naomi had been terrified this would happen ever since her mother died. Her father never wanted her to go to Perkins, and it was only because of her mother that she was able to go. Since her mother died he has been threatening to take her home. He told her Perkins costs too much and they would never teach her anything worth knowing. Her father said she is blind and there is no use pretending she is ever going to be like a regular person.

He wants her to go to a vocational school so she can learn a trade and bring home some money. Naomi said her father loses jobs faster than he gets them because he drinks so much, and now, because of all the trouble in the country, it's even worse.

She begged him to let her stay. She told him all the good things Perkins was doing for her but it is now apparent that her pleas fell on deaf ears.

We are all unbearably distraught. Naomi was one of the nicest girls in the cottage — in the whole school, for that matter. Her being torn from us like this has affected everyone terribly.

Miss Salinger said the play is going to be canceled, which I am thankful for. I would not be able to do it without Naomi.

Ever since they found the Lindbergh baby dead last week, Eva has grown more and more frightened that something will happen to her. Now she thinks the kidnappers are coming to get her next. She has worked herself up into such a state that she hasn't gotten out of bed for the past three days and hasn't eaten anything for the past twenty-four hours.

I wanted to bring some dinner up to her room, but Mrs. Burton said that if Eva wants to eat she has to come down to the dining room and eat there just like everyone else.

First Naomi Walker and now this.

Friday, May 20, 1932

So many awful things have happened I don't even know where to begin.

Eva has a fever and a sore throat and she is worrying so much that she won't be able to sing at the graduation ceremonies that she is making herself sicker and sicker.

Miss Salinger thinks she should take hot baths, but Mama says she shouldn't even go near a bath so I don't know what to do.

"Uncle Ted's Tea" seems to be helping.

I remember when Daddy used to make us drink it if we got sick. Mama says I used to say I'd rather have the sore throat than drink it and Elin used to pour it down the drain when no one was looking.

It's made with tea, honey, lots and lots of garlic, and even more cayenne pepper. It's truly terrible, but it works.

I made Eva some (Mrs. Burton is a little more lenient now that Eva is so sick) and brought it up to her.

I felt her head and unfortunately she still has a very high fever. She has done nothing but sleep all day, sometimes appearing to be delirious.

I tried to get Eva to go see the nurse but she says that if she goes to the nurse she'll send her back, although it isn't really clear back where.

I woke her and made her sit up so she could sip some tea and she said she wanted the special throat lozenges Miss Morgan gave her. She pointed to the bottom drawer of the bureau saying they were in her box.

When I opened the box, there was something carefully wrapped in tissues. Thinking it was the lozenges I unwrapped it and, to my utter amazement, what was revealed within was not the lozenges at all, but Mrs. Burton's long-lost false teeth!

I had to stop myself from screaming. Fortunately Eva had fallen back into one of her fever-induced sleeps.

Just then I heard Amanda's unmistakable skip on the stairs. I didn't know whether I should tell her or not but I did know that I had only seconds to decide.

As it turns out, Amanda already knew. She had suspected Eva from the first because when they were taken she saw Eva get up in the middle of the night, take something out of her skirt pocket, wrap it carefully in tissues, and put it in the box.

In the morning, Amanda stayed behind so she could see if it was what she thought it was, which it was.

Neither of us realized that Eva had awakened and was listening. When she heard what we were talking about she just started screaming, "I hate her! I hate her! I hate her!" over and over and over, rocking back and forth, holding her knees, swaying violently from side to side, and tilting her head heavenward as if praying for divine intervention.

No matter how hard we tried to hold her between us, she would not stop rocking.

Finally, after what seemed like an eternity, her movements slowed and finally subsided until there was only an occasional shudder.

We laid her down on the pillow and she closed her eyes but not before she said in a low voice that seemed to come from deep within her soul, one last time, "I hate her."

Wednesday, May 25, 1932

Eva is better.

Mama and Uncle Ted insisted she come home with me over the weekend.

She is still upset that she might miss her concert and Mama doesn't think she will regain her strength in time (although she has not said this to Eva).

The good news is that she no longer has a fever and Mama has gotten her to eat something.

Sunday, May 29, 1932

Billy asked if I knew about the tunnels. I told him I didn't, which wasn't the whole truth because Amanda knows about them. They're underground passages that connect one cottage with another.

He said he could show me if I wanted but I said I couldn't right now because I had too much home-work, which also wasn't the whole truth.

It's not that I'm afraid of going somewhere alone with Billy. His voice makes me feel the opposite of afraid — safe not scared. But I *am* afraid of disobeying the rules, and I didn't want to tell him that.

Wednesday, June 1, 1932

A most extraordinary turn of events.

Mama and Uncle Ted have decided that Eva is to remain at our house and not return to Perkins until she is fully recovered.

Mama feels that even though Eva is walking around and eating properly she still wants to keep an eye on her.

Uncle Ted is going to speak to the director about it.

Saturday, June 4, 1932

Billy has a big bandage covering his chin. They were playing football and he went out for a pass and ran right into one of the goalposts. He had to be carried to the infirmary on a stretcher because he was unconscious and they were worried that he had a concussion or worse.

I went to visit him in the infirmary. He said he was okay, although he had a really bad headache and was too dizzy to stand up.

He asked me how I lost my sight. No one has ever asked me that before. It was hard to relive that day but I did. I told him all about the accident, and the doctors, and the operations.

Emboldened by his boldness, I asked him what had happened to his eyes. He said he blew out his eyes playing with firecrackers. That's just how he said it and then he laughed, as if to say, "Can you imagine that?"

It all made me think of something Rachel says in the play. "Life is a bitter cup from which we are all forced to drink."

Indeed.

Sunday, June 19, 1932

Miss Margaret Bourke-White spoke at graduation. She is a famous magazine photographer and her mother, Mrs. White, is the housemother at Potter.

She told some funny stories about her mother who, I would imagine, was blushing beet-red throughout the speech.

She said her mother was so strict she wouldn't allow her to play with any children whose parents read comics in the newspapers. (Everyone at Potter says she's still strict, but I doubt anyone can be as bad as Mrs. Burton.)

Her mother taught her to meet life's challenges head on. So Margaret decided when she was our age that she wasn't going to allow being a girl to stop her from doing anything and that we shouldn't allow our blindness to stop us.

"Open all doors," her mother used to tell her and she said the same advice holds true today even if you're blind. "Open those doors and stride right through," she said.

I wish I could be like her. She sounds so bold and determined.

Monday, June 20, 1932

Having Eva stay with us over the summer just makes everything perfect.

Amanda won't be far away, either. Uncle Ted said we might even visit. She is going to the brand-new Perkins summer camp that's on a pond in New Hampshire. There are only twenty girls going and Amanda is really, really excited about it.

I am writing this while sitting on the front porch swing. The birds are splashing and squabbling for position in Mama's birdbath.

Eva and I are going to help Mama care for the garden. Mama has run string up and down so Eva will know where the rows are. I know the paths by heart. This morning I took a walk — I love being in Mama's garden, being alone and smelling the roses.

Inside the house, I can hear Eva and Elin setting the table for dinner. Eva is whistling.

The late afternoon sun casts a warm glow on my face. But, as the seconds tick by, the air is growing chilly as the sun sets. Soon I will have to go in to get warm.

Tuesday, June 21, 1932

It's nice to be home.

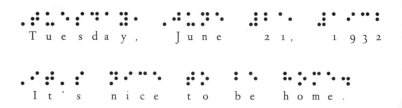

Tuesday, June 21, 1932

It's nice to be home.

Epilogue

Amanda Bright, Eva Anderson, and Bess Brennan remained best friends throughout their years at Perkins, graduating together in June of 1938.

By then, Uncle Ted and Mrs. Brennan had completed the adoption process, which was made even more complicated than usual because there was no Mr. Brennan. By the time Eva became legally adopted she was already considered one of the family.

Three weekday mornings a week, Uncle Ted drove Eva to the Swedish Therapy School in nearby Brookline where she learned the art and technique of massage.

She sang in the church choir and lived with the Brennans for the rest of her life.

In 1933, Bess became aware of and interested in the work of The Seeing Eye, Inc., located in Morristown, New Jersey. The Seeing Eye was the first organization to introduce guide dogs for the blind in the United States. In her junior and senior years Bess had learned typing and other secretarial skills that enabled her to go to work for The Seeing Eye in September of 1939.

She lived in an apartment within walking distance of her job and returned home on weekends. Unlike her sister, Elin, she never married.

Amanda returned to her Nantucket home after graduation. She got a job making beds at the Wauwinet Inn. Sadly, in 1941, while on her father's boat, they were caught in a sudden squall that is believed to have swept them out to sea. They were never heard from again.

Life in America
in 1932

Historical Note

The Perkins School for the Blind opened its doors to the world in July of 1832. Chartered in 1829 as the New England Asylum for the Blind, the Perkins School established serious formal education of the blind in the United States. Before that time, blind children in America were often uneducated and dependent on the charity of others. They had little hope for a future in which they could live as active members of their communities. Described by its first director, Dr. Samuel Gridley Howe, as a place "to give the blind a means of supporting themselves," the Perkins School for the Blind helped to change forever the lives of blind people in the United States.

With only two students and two teachers, the school originally operated out of the home of Dr. Howe's father. The Perkins School continued to grow over the years and eventually admitted deaf-blind children also. The campus changed locations several times, until in 1912 it found its present site in Watertown, Massachusetts.

Before 1832, the Perkins School for the Blind was little more than an idea in the mind of Dr. John Dix Fisher. A native of Boston, Massachusetts, Fisher had visited the National Institution for Blind Youth (*L'Institut national des juenes aveugles*) in Paris as part of his studies in the early 1820s. Opened in 1784, the National Institution for Blind Youth was the first school of its kind anywhere in the world. Fisher was astonished to see the blind students there learning to read, write, and play musical instruments. These, Fisher thought to himself, were blind children who could dream of one day supporting themselves.

When Fisher returned to the United States in 1826, he brought with him a mission to give blind children in America a similar chance. Eventually he gathered together a group of influential friends in a Boston coffeehouse and drew up a plan for what would become America's first school for blind children. In 1831, Dr. Samuel Gridley Howe was chosen as the school's first director, and a year later the school held its first class.

Before 1827, when the first book in Braille was printed, the only way blind people could read was through a printing system known as "embossed type," in which the typeset letters of a text were raised above the surface of the page. A blind person could then "read" the page by running his or her fingertips across the raised letters. It was difficult to read this form of printing because it was hard to tell the letters apart. Thankfully an enterprising young Frenchman named Louis Braille changed that forever, making the printed word easily accessible to the blind.

Born in 1809, Louis Braille lost his sight at the age of four when he accidentally pierced his eye with a sharp tool in his father's workshop. Six years later he was sent to the very same school that would eventually inspire Dr. Fisher to create the Perkins School for the Blind. It was during this time that a soldier named Charles Barbier visited Braille's school with a system of writing called "night writing." It had originally been designed during World War I so that soldiers could pass orders along the trenches at night without giving away their positions. Instead of raised letters, night writing used raised dots and dashes to represent sounds. Unfortunately the system proved too difficult, and was eventually rejected by the military. However, young Louis Braille recognized the value of a system of coded dots over embossed type, especially if it was simplified. Over the next few months, Braille experimented with variations on the original twelve-dot system until he came up with a new method using only six dots, much like the design on a domino. Over the years, he continued perfecting the system that would eventually be named after him, and even developed separate Braille codes for reading math and music. But as remarkable as Braille's system would prove to be, it did not catch on immediately, and for years, embossed type was the best form of reading available to the blind. Today, the Perkins School for the Blind manufactures the Perkins Brailler, a kind of typewriter that enables blind people all over the world to read and write independently in Braille.

In 1837, Dr. Howe admitted a deaf-blind child named Laura Bridgman to the school. Born in 1829,

Bridgman was stricken with scarlet fever just after her second birthday. Though the fever had already taken the lives of her two older sisters, Laura managed to survive — but at a significant cost. Doctors soon discovered that the fever that had killed Laura's siblings had also destroyed her vision and hearing, as well as nearly all her sense of taste and smell. It was under these conditions that Laura Bridgman came to Dr. Howe and the Perkins School for the Blind.

In the 1830s, there was little hope for the life of a deaf-blind person beyond what Howe termed the "darkness and silence of a tomb." She or he was certainly not expected to contribute to society in any meaningful way, let alone possess individual thoughts and feelings. But with Laura Bridgman's arrival at Perkins, Howe had the opportunity to prove the public's perception of the deaf-blind wrong. With Howe's perseverance and faith in the power of education, and her own patience and intelligence, Bridgman would go on to become the first deaf-blind child to be successfully educated. At first through sign language, and later through writing, she learned how to show others what was in her mind. She was able to come out of her shell of isolation and interact with the world around her. The complete and stunning success of her education would pave the way for others to follow.

In 1842, British novelist Charles Dickens visited the Perkins School for the Blind while traveling across the United States. He wrote about his experiences and his visit to the school in his book *American Notes*, in which, more than forty years later, Helen Keller's mother would first learn about the school's existence — and have reason to hope for her daughter's future.

Like Laura Bridgman before her, it is believed that Helen Keller also lost her sight and hearing due to scarlet fever. She was only nineteen months old at the time. For the next seven years, she lived in a world of silence and darkness, growing into a difficult child who had little understanding of the world around her. In 1887, her life would change for the better when Anne Sullivan, a graduate of Perkins, who was herself fully blind by the age of fourteen, came to live with Helen Keller's family, and to teach Helen.

Sullivan had a difficult task in front of her, but unlike Samuel Howe, she had the inspiration of Laura Bridgman's successful education to encourage her. One day, after many weeks of failure, Sullivan hit upon a new way to teach Helen the connection between words and objects. Placing Helen's hand under a spout of running water, Sullivan spelled the letters "w-a-t-e-r" into Helen's other hand. She repeated this several times until suddenly Helen made a connection. All at once she understood that the letters "w-a-t-e-r" meant the refreshing cool something — *water* — that was flowing over her hand. In the next moment, she dropped to the ground and touched the earth, understandably impatient as Sullivan spelled out "e-a-r-t-h" into her hand. By the end of the day, Helen had learned to name a small part of the world now blossoming around her.

From that point on, Helen Keller quickly mastered the ability to communicate both through reading and writing. By 1890, at the age of ten, she decided to overcome the obstacle of speech, which was something almost unheard of for the deaf-blind before then. But as with everything else in her life, Helen succeeded. Continuing to prove that her disabilities would not keep the world out of reach, Keller went on to enter Radcliffe College in 1900, from which she graduated with honors in 1904. For the rest of her life, Helen Keller would use her personal achievements and successes to champion the rights of the disabled the world over.

Today, the Perkins School for the Blind continues strongly in the same vein, providing an education and a way of life for the blind and the deaf-blind. Its halls contain the inspiring stories of countless individuals such as John Dix Fisher, Samuel Howe, Laura Bridgman, Louis Braille, and Helen Keller. Perkins is an example that has allowed numerous schools of its kind to be established around the world.

After visiting L'Institut national des juenes aveugles (National Institution for Blind Youth) in Paris, Dr. John Dix Fisher realized that the United States desperately needed such an institution for blind students. He founded the Perkins School for the Blind in 1829.

Samuel Gridley Howe, the Perkins School's first director, dedicated his career to improving the educational system for blind students. He created textbooks, maps, and other study materials for them. His most famous student, Laura Bridgman, was both blind and deaf. He taught her to write the English alphabet in block letters and to communicate by holding onto a person's hands while he or she spelled out the words. Her successful education proved to the world that deaf-blind people were capable of learning to communicate, and Dr. Howe's pioneering in this field led to an educational revolution.

Helen Keller, who is pictured here reading a book at the Perkins School, lost her sight, hearing, and speech at the age of nineteen months due to a severe illness.

When Helen Keller was six years old, Anne Sullivan, (pictured right), also blind and a recent Perkins graduate, came to be her live-in tutor. Anne taught her to read Braille and to write in English. With Anne's life-long tutelage, Helen enrolled at Perkins and went on to graduate from Radcliffe College in 1904.

Louis Braille, born near Paris in 1809, was blinded at the age of three. While he attended a school for blind children, he learned "night writing." Using raised dots to create words, this system was designed for soldiers posted in trenches, who needed to pass messages at night. Braille experimented with this method, and simplified it, creating the Braille Alphabet for the Blind.

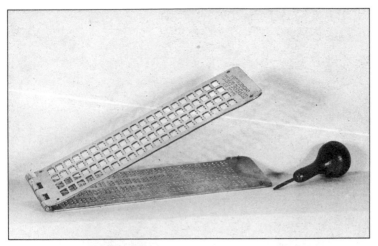

In the 1930s, students at the Perkins School wrote in Braille using a Braille slate, in which paper is inserted, and a stylus, which is used to punch the raised dots. Though it is read from left to right, Braille is written from right to left, as the raised dots appear on the reverse side of the paper.

Students use the Perkins Brailler in a classroom at the Perkins School in the 1950s. A mechanical Braille writer, the Perkins Brailler was invented in 1951 by David Abraham, a former teacher at the Perkins School. Newer versions of the Perkins Brailler are still used today.

A tactile globe, created at the Perkins School in the 1830s, was used in classrooms through the 1930s to teach geography to blind students.

Students in the 1930s play in the snow in front of Bradlee Cottage and ice-skate on the pond at the Perkins School for the Blind.

In the early 1940s, students at the Perkins School for the Blind Upper School for Girls eat in the dining area of one of the cottages.

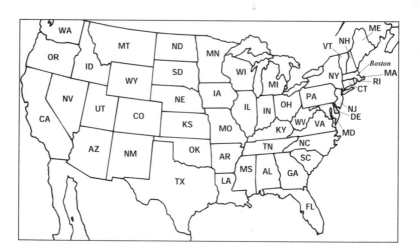

Map of the United States, highlighting Boston, Massachusetts.

About the Author

Barry Denenberg is the author of several critically acclaimed books for young readers, including four books in the Dear America series, *Early Sunday Morning: The Pearl Harbor Diary of Amber Billows*; *When Will This Cruel War Be Over?: The Civil War Diary of Emma Simpson*, which was named an NCSS Notable Children's Trade Book in the Field of Social Studies and a YALSA Quick Pick; *One Eye Laughing, the Other Weeping: The Diary of Julie Weiss*; and *So Far from Home: The Diary of Mary Driscoll, an Irish Mill Girl*, and two books in the My Name Is America series, *The Journal of William Thomas Emerson: A Revolutionary War Patriot*, and *The Journal of Ben Uchida, Citizen 13559, Mirror Lake Internment Camp*. Praised for his meticulous research, Barry Denenberg has written books about diverse times in American history, from the Civil War to Vietnam.

Denenberg's nonfiction works include *An American*

Hero: The True Story of Charles A. Lindbergh, which was named an ALA Best Book for Young Adults, and a New York Public Library Book for the Teen Age; *Voices from Vietnam*, an ALA Best Book for Young Adults, a *Booklist* Editor's Choice, and a New York Public Library Book for the Teen Age; and *All Shook Up: The Life and Death of Elvis Presley*. He lives with his wife and their daughter in Westchester County, New York.

Dedicated to Cafer Barkus

Acknowledgments

The author would like to thank Kristen Eberle, Kerry Balassone, Cafer Barkus, Amy Griffin, Beth Levine, Doug Barker, Al and Betty Gazaygian, June Tuligankas, Larry Melander, Lisa Sandell, Kerrie Baldwin, and Manuela Soares.

Grateful acknowledgment is made for permission to reprint the following:

Cover Portrait: Bettman/CORBIS.
Cover Background: Courtesy of Larry Melander, The Perkins School for the Blind.

Page 127: Dr. John Dix Fisher, The Perkins School for the Blind.
Page 128 (top): Dr. Samuel Gridley Howe, The Perkins School for the Blind.
Page 128 (bottom): Dr. Howe and Laura Bridgman, The Perkins School for the Blind.
Page 129 (top): Helen Keller at the Perkins School, The Perkins School for the Blind.
Page 129 (bottom): Helen Keller and Anne Sullivan, Brown Brothers.
Page 130: Louis Braille, Bettmann/CORBIS.
Page 131 (top): Braille slate and stylus, Brown Brothers.
Page 131 (bottom): Perkins Brailler, The Perkins School for the Blind.
Page 132: Tactile globe, The Perkins School for the Blind.
Page 133 (top): Perkins students playing in the snow, The Perkins School for the Blind.
Page 133 (bottom): Perkins students ice-skating, The Perkins School for the Blind.
Page 134 (top): Perkins School dining hall, The Perkins School for the Blind.
Page 134 (bottom): Map by Heather Saunders.

Other books by Barry Denenberg

All Shook Up
The Life and Death of Elvis Presley

Other Dear America books
by Barry Denenberg

When Will This Cruel War Be Over?
The Civil War Diary of Emma Simpson

So Far from Home
The Diary of Mary Driscoll, An Irish Mill Girl

One Eye Laughing, the Other Weeping
The Diary of Julie Weiss

Early Sunday Morning
The Pearl Harbor Diary of Amber Billows

My Name Is America books
by Barry Denenberg

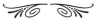

The Journal of William Thomas Emerson
A Revolutionary War Patriot

The Journal of Ben Uchida
Citizen 1 3559, Mirror Lake Internment Camp

Copyright © 2002 by Barry Denenberg

꒰ ꒱

All rights reserved. Published by Scholastic Inc.
DEAR AMERICA®, SCHOLASTIC, and associated logos are trademarks
and/or registered trademarks of Scholastic Inc.

Library of Congress Cataloging-in-Publication Data

Denenberg, Barry.
Mirror, mirror on the wall: the diary of Bess Brennan / by Barry Denenberg.
p. cm. — (Dear America)
Summary: In 1932, a twelve-year-old girl who lost her sight in an accident
keeps a diary, recorded by her twin sister, in which she describes life at
Perkins School for the Blind in Watertown, Massachusetts.
ISBN 0-439-19446-6
[1. Perkins Institution and Massachusetts School for the Blind — Fiction.
2. Blind — Fiction. 3. Physically handicapped — Fiction.
4. Twins — Fiction. 5. Diaries — Fiction.
6. United States — History — 1919–1933 — Juvenile fiction.
7. United States — History — 1919–1933 — Fiction.]
I. Title. II. Series.
PZ7.D4135 Mi 2002
[Fic] — 21   2001049796
CIP AC

10 9 8 7 6 5 4 3 2 1   02 03 04 05 06

The display type was set in Locarno Light.
The text type was set in DeepdeneH.
Book design by Elizabeth B. Parisi
Photo research by Dwayne Howard

Printed in the U.S.A.   23
First edition, September 2002

꒰ ꒱

106776 LMR   FIC DENE